Immortal
Max

Lutricia Clifton

Holiday House / New York

Acknowledgments

Special thanks to my editor, Julie Amper,

and the other amazingly talented, hardworking people

at Holiday House who made this book possible.

Being part of the Holiday House family is truly a privilege.

Thanks also to my friend Barbara Flores,

who told me about a dog named Carl,

the inspiration for this book.

HOLIDAY HOUSE is registered in the U.S. Patent and Trademark Office.
Printed and Bound in December 2013 at Maple Press, York, PA, USA.
www.holidayhouse.com
First Edition
1   3   5   7   9   10   8   6   4   2

Library of Congress Cataloging-in-Publication Data
Clifton, Lutricia.
Immortal Max / by Lutricia Clifton. — First edition.
pages cm
Summary: Twelve-year-old Sammy's summer is full of complications, but he comes
to appreciate what he already has even as he is working toward his long-held dream
of owning a purebred puppy.
ISBN 978-0-8234-3041-3 (hardcover)
[1. Dogs—Fiction.   2. Brothers and sisters—Fiction.   3. Moneymaking
projects—Fiction.   4. Single-parent families—Fiction.]   I. Title.
PZ7.C622412Imm 2014
[Fic]—dc23
2013023664

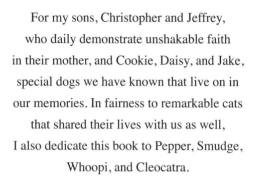

For my sons, Christopher and Jeffrey,
who daily demonstrate unshakable faith
in their mother, and Cookie, Daisy, and Jake,
special dogs we have known that live on in
our memories. In fairness to remarkable cats
that shared their lives with us as well,
I also dedicate this book to Pepper, Smudge,
Whoopi, and Cleocatra.

Chapter 1

Come on, guys—*Hurry up....*

The clock ticking. Time running out. I'm waiting for my turn, and the other kids are taking their sweet time. There's just this one last thing to do before summer vacation starts, and it's almost time for last bell.

I'm always next to last. Justin comes after me because his last name's Wysocki. Mine's Smith. Sammy Smith. But mostly, I'm called *Spammy* Smith. Why? Because that's how my cute baby sister pronounced it when she was learning to talk. My clever older sister made it my nickname. Sam became Spam. Spam became Spammy.

Chopped ham in a can.

There's three of us. Two sisters, no brothers. My older sister, Elizabeth—called Beth—is seventeen and leaving for college in the fall. She's the brainiac. After she finishes college, she wants to go to vet school. Roseanne—Rosie for short—is six going on seven. She wants to be a...well, that changes week to week, sometimes day to day. But it usually involves a tutu. And then there's me. Sandwich filling between a multigrain bagel and a French pastry.

"Well now, let's see who's next." Mrs. Kellogg sifts through the class roll. She wears these lined glasses that make things different sizes. Finally, she finds the right line on her glasses and says, "Yee, it's your turn."

No one could believe it. Our last day in elementary school and we're assigned a show-and-tell. *Bring in your collection,* Mrs.

Kellogg told us. *Or talk about your hobby, what you plan to do on your summer vacation. You know, something special.*

Yee Haan all but disappears behind the huge map of East Asia she holds up. Almond eyes peeking over a paper fence. She's going to see her grandparents in August.

She points out a tiny speck off the coast of China called Taiwan, also known as the Republic of China. She's always talking about being Chinese American. Of course, she has to explain the difference between the Republic of China and the People's Republic of China, how her grandparents escaped during the revolution, and how her parents immigrated to the United States and became naturalized citizens.

"I was born in Chicago," she says, smiling. "That means I'm a natural-born citizen."

I was ready to escape from *both* Chinas long before Yee reached Chicago. The clock on the wall ticks like a time bomb. I'm never going to get my turn.

But Yee's not done yet. Everyone *ooh*s and *ahh*s when she brings out her passport because they've never seen one before.

"Pass it around," Mrs. Kellogg tells her.

"Well, the picture's not very good...." Yee hesitates, looking reluctant, then says, "Okay, as long as you don't laugh."

Yee has the prettiest hair of all the girls. Long shiny black hair. She's the most serious girl in class, too. You can tell that from her haircut. Straight-cut bangs. Straight-cut edges that brush her shoulders. And *never* a hair out of place. I grin when Yee's passport reaches me. Her hair has been pushed behind her ears so her moon-round face will show better. She stares back at me with furious eyes and pinched lips. Number one on the FBI's Most Outraged Juvie list.

"Oh...." Yee pauses, looking as excited as a serious person can look. "And I'm going to cheer camp so I can become a cheerleader. Because I'm a little person, I just know I'll be the top of the pyramid."

Top of the pyramid? Then I get it. It's that thing cheerleaders do to make a human triangle with their bodies.

Glancing around sneaky-like, Yee whispers, "But my grand-parents can't know because they don't approve of such things. So don't say anything to them. Okay?"

What? We're going to call them in Taiwan?

"Sidharth," Mrs. Kellogg says when Yee sits down. "You're next."

Sidharth Patel—Sid for short—brought his pet gerbil. "We are going nowhere this summer," he says, "so I will have plenty of time to play with George. That's his name, George the Gerbil."

Yee jumps to her feet, waving a finger at Sid. "It's disrespect-ful to give an animal a person's name."

Mrs. Kellogg decides that Yee should explain her culture's belief. Mrs. Kellogg lucked out and got three kids in her class with different cultural backgrounds this year, not white bread like the rest of us, so we're always learning how they look at things.

Yee tells us how the Chinese name pets for their person-alities. How the Chinese zodiac features twelve animals. How years are named for a zodiac animal, and how people born in an animal's year will be bestowed with its characteristics. Five minutes later, she sits down. Again.

"All right...." Mrs. Kellogg pauses, looking at Sid. "Now explain the beliefs in your country about naming animals, Sidharth."

This is Sid's first year in the United States. He was born in India and speaks English like a news commentator on the BBC. I figure Mrs. Kellogg is thinking about sacred cows, which Sid has told us are allowed to walk around wherever they want.

"I don't know much about naming cows...." He's figured out she's thinking about sacred cows, too. "But my father told me that once, there were cows in every household. It was because cows are the givers of milk and important for survival." He glances at Yee. "I believe they were considered part of the family and given regular names."

Yee closes up like a clam. Scowling.

"That's all I know." Sid looks at Mrs. Kellogg. "I didn't have a cow when we lived in India. And here I can only have a small pet, which I can never let out of its cage. If George escapes, our guests will think we have rats and won't stay with us."

"*Oh*, that's right. You live at the hotel on the highway."

Our school's on the edge of town. It's the kind of town that's not too big and not too small. A movie theater on the square. A McDonald's and a DQ. A Walmart and Farm & Fleet, where mostly country people shop. And the Midwest Jewel Inn.

"Yes, my family is in the hotel business. It's our bread and butter. We live in rooms behind the check-in desk. George lives with us…in his cage."

Yee's hand pops into the air again, but Mrs. Kellogg ignores it. Her way of calling a cease-fire in the cultural war between China and India.

"George is cool," I whisper as Sid returns to his desk.

"Thanks, Sam."

Sid is a mealy kid, pale and weak looking, like oatmeal, but he's Kid Genius in the classroom and kicks butt on the soccer field. He's not a show-off, though. He's the kind of guy my grandpa would've said had "substance."

"Anise, I believe you're next."

Anise Pierce shows us a brochure of Disney World, where her family is vacationing this summer. Last year, they went to Disneyland. The year before, Six Flags over Texas. I don't know where they went before that because she didn't live here then. But I'm sure it had a *humongous* water slide, a *humongous* roller coaster, or a *humongous* something else. *Humongous* is Anise's favorite word. She uses it to describe something that's over the top. She finally finishes comparing Space Mountain with Splash Mountain and walks toward her desk.

"*Oh….*" She pushes coffee-brown hair out of her eyes. "And my mom named us after spices that match the color of our skin. The dried seeds, not the plants, which are always green. That's how I got to be named Anise and my sister Saffron. She's yellower than I am. My brother's name is Mace. Mama didn't know

4

what color that was, but it sounded like a good spice name for a boy."

I don't know what color mace is, either. Or saffron, for that matter. But I know what color anise is now. Creamy brown, like peanut butter.

"*And*—" Anise looks at Yee, clapping her hands. Something she does when she's about to make an exciting announcement. "I'm going to cheerleading camp, too, so we can practice together! I took modern dance when we lived in the burbs and am really good at whirls and spins."

A lot of the kids in my class moved from the suburbs—what they call the burbs—to CountryWood Estates, the new gated community outside town. Their parents work from home on computers or do videoconferencing. Anise's dad even teaches school on the computer. My grandpa laughed when the houses started going up. He said people used to move to the city to find work, but now things were ass backward. He was right. These days, BMWs and minivans play bumper cars with John Deere tractors and International Harvesters.

Bailey Powell is up next. She lives across the road from me. She's wearing her favorite shoes, Dr. Seuss Converse high-tops with the Cat in the Hat on the toes. She makes most of her clothes because she wants to be a clothes designer. Today she's wearing grape-colored crop pants that bunch up between her thighs and a pink tee with green sequins on the front that spell HUG ME. I asked her once why she dressed so weird, and she said she didn't want to be a Cliché. That's what she calls the CountryWood kids, who mostly wear skinny jeans and T-shirts with words like AERO-POSTALE and WET SEAL on the front. But I know she was lying. She melts like an ice cube when a Burbie speaks to her.

Aww, man. I can't believe it when Bailey carries two boxes to the front. I'm betting she brought her whole Barbie doll collection—*and* the outfits she designed herself.

"*Snickerdoodles.*" Bailey opens the first box. "I made cookies for everyone!"

"Wait." Mrs. Kellogg holds up her hand like a crossing guard. "You're not supposed to have fattening treats."

"No, it's okay. Mama helped me bake them last night. It's my last big splurge 'cause I'm gonna lose a ton of weight this summer."

Bailey's been trying to lose weight since I've known her, which is forever. She's one of the kids who was actually born here, like me. Her mother's been on a rip since the talk about obesity in kids has been in the news. But I think Bailey has a different reason for losing weight.

"Your mother usually sends me a note...." Mrs. Kellogg hesitates, her neck sagging. She has this flap of skin under her chin like a chicken's wattle that jiggles when her head moves. "Oh, what the heck," she mumbles, neck waggling. "It's the last day of school. Pass them around and take your seat."

"But I'm not done yet." Bailey opens the second box and takes out two pom-poms. Purple and orange, the colors of the middle school athletic teams. "I'm going to cheerleading camp, too, so we can all practice together!" She flashes Yee and Anise her smiley-face grin. "I've already learned one cheer."

Before Mrs. Kellogg can stop her, Bailey starts shaking the pom-poms over her head and down at the floor, yelling:

"We're number one,
Can't be number two,
And we're going to beat
The *whoops* out of you!"

Bailey jumps up and down when she's done, making her stomach shake like blubber.

"Cheerleading camp?" Justin makes snorting sounds like a pig. "You need to go to a fat farm!"

Bailey's skin is snow white and covered in big brown freckles, and when she blushes, she turns bright red. Right now, she's a strawberry sundae sprinkled with chocolate chips. She keeps on smiling her smiley face, though. Like always.

"That's enough!" Mrs. Kellogg rubs her face hard, like she's erasing the whiteboard. "Pass out the cookies, Bailey."

I watch Bailey carry the box of cookies up and down rows, laying two on her own desk, and shake my head.

We work through the rest of the P and R names, then it's my turn. There aren't any kids whose names begin with Q.

"Please hurry, Samuel. We're almost out of time."

She's telling *me* to hurry?

Rushing up front, I hold up a three-ring binder. "This is a scrapbook I've been working on since I was seven. My older sister got me started on it." I point out SAM'S DOG BOOK printed on the front with a felt-tip marker and pictures of dogs under the plastic cover. "I've been learning about dogs for years—purebred dogs—and saving so I can buy a puppy." I flip open the cover and turn pages so the class can see the pictures and descriptions of dogs. "And I'm going to train it, too. I already know how 'cause I practiced on Max. That's why he minds me better than anyone else. And..."

I look around the class, about to explode.

"I've finally saved enough money! I had a hard time deciding what kind to get, but I narrowed it down to a German shepherd. I can't get the puppy just yet, but soon as I can, I'm going to buy one—"

"Wait, Samuel." Mrs. Kellogg does the crossing guard thing with her hand again. "If you've saved enough money, why can't you buy a puppy now?"

"What? Oh, because of Max."

"Who's Max?"

"The old dog that lives with us."

"That big shaggy dog that walks you to the bus stop?" Anise blinks slow, like she's looking at a picture in her head. "The one that waits for you when school is over?"

"Uh, yeah."

"Shouldn't name a dog after a person," Yee mumbles. "It's disrespectful."

"We know, we know." Mrs. Kellogg's eyes are glazing over.

"Is Max sick?" Bailey looks worried. "He's not about to die, is he?"

"Yes—No—what I mean is, not exactly. He was sick when Beth brought him home. *Real* sick. Everyone at the shelter figured his days were numbered. He'd stopped eating, was skinny as a beanpole."

"Why did Beth bring him home?" Mrs. Kellogg knows who Beth is because she taught her years ago.

" 'Cause that's the kind of dumb thing she does. Which is why we have six cats—no, seven. She brought another one home last night."

Mrs. Kellogg raises an eyebrow, a signal I need to explain.

"See, Beth works part-time at a vet hospital and volunteers at an animal shelter, and when animals don't get adopted, they get euthanized. So Beth brings them home. The cats, anyway. They mostly live in the shed where Mom stores flower seed and straw for mulching. They eat the mice, which keeps the place clean and saves on cat food."

"Eeeww." Anise's face screws up like she just tasted something bad. "Your cats eat mice?"

"What's *euthanized* mean?" Bailey's eyebrows pinch together.

"Killed, stupid! Iced. Terminated." Pretending he's slicing his throat, Justin chokes out *"Kaput."* For some reason, he finds that funny.

Justin is a soft kid with a round face and hair gelled up like a push broom. Even though he's shorter than me, he makes me feel small. Hobbit small. And he laughs like a hyena, a cackling howl.

"Well, yes," Mrs. Kellogg tells Bailey. "It means the animal is put to sleep." She looks at me. "Are you saying that Max was scheduled to be euthanized, Samuel?"

"Yeah. So Beth brought him home to spend his final days with us. He was supposed to be on his last legs."

"How long has he been on his last legs?" Yee asks. She's wearing her summer uniform. Polo shirt and roll-top Bermudas. Crew socks and white Adidas, polished. Miss Neatnik.

"Well, uh, four years. He got better."

"Four years?" Sid's eyes open wide "A *miracle* dog."

"Immortal Max," Justin howls. "The dog that refused to die."

Mrs. Kellogg fires Justin a look, then turns to me. "That doesn't explain why you can't buy your puppy now, Samuel."

"Yeah," Yee says. "I have two Pekingese. My vet says pets do better in pairs."

" 'Cause Mom says so. Max is old, and she's afraid a puppy would be too hard on him."

"Poor Max." Anise's eyes melt like warm chocolate. "No one wanted him."

Everyone looks sad. Instead of being excited for me, they're feeling sorry for Max.

"Thank you, Samuel. I believe we have just enough time to see what Justin has brought."

"But I didn't get to tell you how much money I've saved."

"All right then, but be quick."

"One . . . hundred . . . dollars—"

"A hundred dollars!" A hyena laugh echoes from the back of the classroom. "My dog cost *four* hundred dollars."

"Four hundred dollars!" I feel like someone just punched me in the gut. "You're lying, Justin. Puppies don't cost that much—"

"Check the want ads, Spammy. You won't find a dog—a purebred dog—for a hundred bucks."

Silence. Except for the clock.

"Well, my poodle *did* cost more than a hundred dollars," Anise says. "We call him Midnight because he's black."

"And my Pekingese cost more than that, too. Their names are Rooster and Rabbit, to describe their personalities." Yee, the Chinese zodiac expert, gives Sid a look. *"That's* the way it's done in China."

"My gerbil cost nine dollars and ninety-eight cents. He was on sale at PetSmart. His name is George. George the Gerbil—"

"No more about *names.*" Mrs. Kellogg sighs, pushes her glasses up her nose, and looks at Justin. "The price would depend on the breed, Justin. What kind of dog do you have? Maybe Samuel is getting a different kind."

"German shepherd, a sable-colored German shepherd named Bruno. He has a pedigree this long." Justin stretches his arm out as long as he can make it.

Sable German shepherd! No way—that's the kind of puppy I've decided on.

Twenty-eight sets of eyes staring at me. The clock ticking. My mouth refusing to make words.

"Samuel, do you have anything else to say? You must hurry. It's almost time for last bell, and Justin needs his turn."

"Uh, no. I'm done." I close my dog book with a *smack* and walk toward my desk. I feel like crying or hitting something.

As we pass, Justin bumps me, making me drop the binder.

"Hey, swerve man." I shove him back. "Don't come at me all reckless."

"Then steer clear, *Spammy*." He shoulders past me.

Justin is the biggest show-off in class. Just once, I wish someone would cut him down to size. Besides, everyone already knows what he plans to talk about. *Black Ops II* for his Xbox. He's been talking about it for weeks.

But it's not *Black Ops II*. Justin shows off keys to a new golf cart his dad just bought *and* which he gets to drive all summer.

"It's gasoline powered so it can really fly. It's a lot faster than our old one. Those golf carts that run on batteries are gutless."

"But where are you going to drive it, Justin?" Mrs. Kellogg's distorted eyes look confused. "Golf carts aren't allowed on the roads, and I don't believe there's a golf course at CountryWood."

"Yeah, there's not. But I can take it to the beach at the lake and the tennis courts and the swimming pool and—"

"I'm sure you'll enjoy it." Mrs. Kellogg looks at the clock again. "Take your seat now."

"But I haven't told you how much it cost," Justin says, pretending to whine. "You let Spammy tell how much he's going to pay for a purebred puppy."

"Oh, all right. And refer to him as Samuel, his proper name."

Justin grins. "I like Spammy better."

Bailey groans. Yee and Anise roll their eyes. My face turns into a fireball.

"*Sit.*" Mrs. Kellogg jabs a finger at Justin's desk. His walking orders.

"*Twenty-five big ones.*" As Justin passes my desk, he dangles the keys to the golf cart in front of my nose. "That's twenty... five...hundred dollars, *Spammy.*" A cackling howl ricochets off the walls.

"Know what your nickname is, Justin?" Yee's eyes are sparking. "It's *Jerk* with a capital *J*. Justin the Jerk!"

"Yeah. Justin the *Humongous* Jerk," Anise echoes.

"Hey, wait!" Justin stops in the middle of the aisle, grinning like a monkey. "I just thought of a new nickname for *Samuel.*" He makes an *L* with his thumb and index finger and holds it to his face like it's a brand burned on his forehead. "Spammy the *Loser,* who will never get a purebred puppy."

"Will, too!" I'm on my feet in a flash. Face hot. Fists clenched. "And I'm going to buy it this summer. A German shepherd puppy."

"Oh, yeah? And just how are you gonna do that, Spammy? Helping your mama sell petunias?"

Burbies laugh. Even some of the Townies.

I sink into my chair, a deflated balloon.

"*Enough!*" Mrs. Kellogg shouts. "Everyone, pack up your things *now.*"

Sid jumps to his feet as the last bell rings. "May I hand these out, Mrs. Kellogg? It is a very big deal for my family."

"What?" She glances at the slip he hands her. "Oh, I suppose, but make it quick."

Sid passes out yellow slips that no one reads because they're ready to escape. I stuff mine into my backpack as Mrs. Kellogg says, "Class dismissed. Good luck in middle school!"

Kids rush for the door, laughing and yelling. Except me. The last thing I do as an elementary student is throw my scrapbook in the trash. Justin was right. It took me years to save a hundred dollars. There's no way I can earn another three hundred before summer is over.

I *am* a loser.

Chapter 2

Kids jam onto the school bus. Yelling. Laughing. Throwing wadded candy wrappers and punching each other on the arm. I stuff my backpack under the seat and stare out the window, watching grasshoppers perform belly flops and trying to shut out end-of-year conversations.

"Did Spammy tell you 'bout my new kitten?" My little sister, Rosie, sits down next to Bailey. They're across the aisle from me, like always.

There's a pecking order on the bus. Those of us who get off first sit up front. Sid has the shortest ride because the hotel is nearest the school. Bailey lives across the road from us, so she gets off with Rosie and me. The Burbies sit at the back, except for Anise and Yee. They're different from the other Burbies, not so full of themselves. They live next door to each other at Country-Wood, too, so they chummed up right away.

"Don't call me *Spammy*," I growl across the aisle.

Rosie's grin slides off her face.

"Let's call him Sammy, okay?" Catching my eye, Bailey gives me her smiley face. "He told the whole class about your new kitten," she tells Rosie. "He said you have *seven* cats now. What are you gonna name this one?"

"Selena."

Yee makes a choking sound. She and Anise are sitting in the seat behind me.

"That sounds like a Cliché's name," Bailey says. "I bet we can come up with something better than that."

"Like what?"

All at once, Bailey gets all bouncy. "I know! Robinson Crusoe named a man Friday 'cause that was the day he found him. You have seven cats now, so you could name them after the days of the week. What day did you get your new kitten?"

"You mean, name it Thursday?" Rosie's mouth opens in a snaggle-toothed grin. "Yeah, I can change *all* of their names to days of the week 'cause we have seven cats and there are seven days in a week."

"*Awesome.*" Bailey pulls a snickerdoodle out of her backpack and hands it to Rosie. "Here, I saved this for you."

Aww, man. Major slip-up. Bailey wasn't going to eat that extra cookie. She saved it for Rosie. I mouth "Thanks" across the aisle and get another smiley-face grin.

Sid climbs on the bus and sits down next to me. Setting George's cage between his feet, he pulls my scrapbook out of his backpack. "I think you will regret throwing this away," he says. "It was a really big deal for you."

"You can kiss that good-bye," I say, groaning. "I'll never have enough money to buy a pedigreed puppy."

"A pity." He pauses, looking thoughtful. "Then keep it as a dream book."

"A what?"

"A book for holding your dreams." He pushes the scrapbook into my hands. "I have always wanted a little Chihuahua, but it would look too much like a rat. I'm also afraid it would bark a lot. I'm told that Chihuahuas have nervous dispositions."

"Yeah, that's what I heard, too."

"So you see, I can't have one. But I would love a book like this, just to dream about the day I could get one."

That's what I was trying to tell the class....

"Thanks." I stuff the dog book into my backpack and shove it back under the seat. "It *is* kind of special."

Outside the bus, Townies pair up or form small clusters to walk home. Crunching across worn-out grass. Talking about stopping somewhere to celebrate summer vacation, like McDonald's or DQ. Big deal. My stop will be the refrigerator for a soda pop. An *ice*-cold soda pop. The bus is an oven. Suddenly, someone nudges me on the shoulder.

"Why can't you earn the extra money you need to buy a dog?" Bailey says. Eavesdropping, of course.

"You're sitting next to it." I nod at Rosie. "Have to watch *her* when Mom's working."

Summer is Mom's busiest time. After my dad was killed in a car accident, she opened up a plant nursery in an old shed next to the house. We live halfway between town and CountryWood, a good location for her business. She has a big garden plot out back for growing perennials, plants that come back every year like daylilies and daisies. And she plants seeds in flowerpots early in the spring for annuals, which can't survive cold winters. Geraniums and petunias mostly. A lot of customers come back to buy from her, and sometimes she plants the flowers for them. From time to time, she even does workshops, teaching people how to care for their gardens.

"I babysit for people on weekends," Bailey says. "That's how I bought my pom-poms. Mom's paying for cheerleading camp 'cause she wants me to lose twenty pounds. She figures I'll sweat it off if I do cheers." She glances out the window as the bus starts up. "She's probably right. It's dumb hot out there and summer just started."

"Yeah, well. Mom can't afford to pay me, and there's no way I'm going to babysit other people's brats. One is enough."

"You called me a brat." Rosie's bottom lip starts to quiver. Jell-O in a fleshy mold.

"He didn't call *you* a brat." Bailey looks at me. "Did you, Sammy?"

"Yeah, whatever."

"See..." Bailey smiles at Rosie. "He wasn't talking about you."

A sigh slips out of my mouth. Bailey's the eternal optimist. Sappy. Why doesn't she get it? Things aren't always good. Sometimes you just have to wake up. I go back to looking out the smeary window.

"What's a petty-greed dog?" Rosie asks, spewing cookie crumbs.

"Ped-i-greed." Bailey spells the word for her. "It's a dog with papers."

"What kind of papers?"

"A pedigree is like a birth certificate. Only for dogs."

"Why can't cats have birth certificates?"

"Oh, I guess cats can, too." Bailey looks at me again. "So do something other than babysit."

"Like what?" I snort. "It took me years to save a hundred dollars from the allowance Mom gives me and the odd jobs Grandpa paid me to do. Now that he's gone, I don't have a way to earn extra money." I cross my arms and go back to staring out the window. "There just aren't any jobs for a twelve-year-old kid around here."

"Then make one," Yee says.

Yee's the smartest kid in class, next to Sid. I've never seen anyone who works so hard at being smart as she does. But this is the dumbest thing that's ever come out of her mouth.

"Make a job?" I twist in my seat so I can see behind me. "You can't just *make* a job."

"Sure you can. What do you know a lot about?"

"Dogs!" Justin yells from the back of the bus. "*Dog Boy* knows all about dogs."

He must have amplifiers in his ears to hear us over the noise. The other Burbies are yak-yakking like crazy, taking pictures of each other with iPhones, laughing and yelling. A three-ring circus.

"Mind your own business!" Bailey yells at him.

"No," Yee says. "Justin's right. You *do* know a lot about dogs, Sammy. You could watch dogs instead of kids."

"Babysit dogs?"

"Sure. When people go away on vacation, they have some-one come in to take care of their dogs. Cats, too. You know, feed and water them."

"Or you could *walk* dogs," Anise says. "Some of our neighbors are so old, I bet they'd pay someone to exercise their dogs for them."

"That's even better." Yee's eyes start to blink slow, like they're mechanized. "That way, you could set up a schedule."

"You know what *exercising* means, Dog Boy?" Justin has moved closer to the front. He's three rows back now. "Being a *pooper scooper*. Picking up woof-woof waste."

Yee and Anise roll their eyes at each other.

"Picking up poop?" Bailey raises her eyebrows. "Why don't they just put their dogs in the backyard? That's what we do. That way, the dog would get exercise and they'd only have to pick up poop every three or four days." She screws up her face. "That's one of my jobs."

" 'Cause we're not allowed to have fences around our yards," Anise says, "and it's against the law to let dogs run loose. Some people put their dogs on tie-outs instead of walking them...." She gives Justin a look. "But no matter where they poop, you're still *supposed* to pick up after them."

That look says a lot. Justin doesn't play by the rules. Big surprise.

"I don't understand," Bailey says. "The whole place is fenced. I know 'cause Mom drives by there when we go see my grandparents."

Bailey's right, I've seen it, too. A six-foot PVC fence surrounds CountryWood. A wall of big white plastic panels. All you can see are rooftops over the top.

"Oh," Anise says. "The fence is for privacy—and security."

"Security?" I look at Anise like her brain sprang a leak. "Like that fence is supposed to keep someone out? Geez, I could get over it like *that*." I pop a finger snap.

"Sammy..." Leaning close, Yee whispers, "There's been a problem with vandalism. Everyone thinks it's Townies."

"*Hey.*" Justin stands up, yelling to the Burbies at the back of the bus. "Did you hear that? Spammy said he's been climbing over the fence at CountryWood."

"Did *not*. I was just...just..."

"I believe Sammy was making a point," Sid says.

"Yeah, making a point."

"The *point* is, we can't let our dogs run free." Anise gives Justin another look. "We're supposed to keep them on a leash when we take them outside. But *some* people keep their dogs in a crate all day long. No wonder they go crazy when they're finally let out."

Go crazy? Is she talking about Justin's dog?

"A crate?" Rosie says. "You mean, like a wooden box?"

"No, a *wire* crate. We put Midnight in one when we go shopping 'cause Mom doesn't want the house messed up."

"We have one for Rooster and Rabbit, too. Because they're small, they share one."

"But that's so *mean*." Bailey's eyebrows bunch up. "We have a fenced backyard for our dog. She's a blond cocker spaniel... well, mostly cocker." She flashes her toothy grin at Yee. "Her name's Blondie."

Another sigh slips out. I hate it when Bailey tries to make a Burbie like her. Like, not naming her dog after a person will make Yee her best friend?

"It is *not* mean." Yee's tone is indignant, like she's been insulted. "Animal psychologists say dogs like to be kept in crates. It's their den. You know, like when they used to be wild."

I let out a louder sigh. "Oh, so now you're a *dog* psychologist, too?"

Yee's dad is a psychologist, the kind that does research. She's always analyzing everything and everyone.

"No." Yee looks at me. "My vet told me."

"Well, all I know is Max wasn't happy in a cage. That's why Beth brought him home to live with us."

"Oh, I don't know." Sid glances at George. "Living in a cage isn't so bad."

"There's no way Spammy could exercise dogs." Justin has commandeered the seat behind Bailey and Rosie now. "We have *rules*."

"What kind of rules?" Bailey twists in her seat so she can see Justin, Yee, and Anise.

"All kinds," Anise says. "That's why my parents moved here. The gangs had gotten really bad in the city, and after Saffron…"

As Anise's voice trails off, Yee pats her on the arm.

"The fence is to keep scum out," Justin says, taking over again. "That's why Townies have to get a pass to get in the security gate. Besides, we're talking *expensive* dogs. People aren't going to trust just anyone with them. People steal expensive dogs, you know."

"Spammy's not a stealer," Rosie says.

"Sammy," Bailey whispers.

"Sammy's not a stealer," Rosie says again.

"No, he's right." Just once, I wish Justin would be wrong about something. "Who's going to trust a twelve-year-old kid with an expensive dog?"

Which I will never have.

"One with credentials." Sid indicates my backpack.

"Yeah, you know more about dogs than anyone I know, but…" Bailey's forehead wrinkles up like she's thinking real deep. "How would people know you're in the dog exercising business?"

"Don't you mean woof-woof waste collector?" Hyena giggles ricochet off the bus windows. *A-heh-heh-heh-heh-heh.*

Yee and Anise put their heads together, whispering, and follow with a look at me.

What's going on?

The bus slows. The sign on the side pops out, warning motorists to stop. Sid stands up, holding George's cage, ready to exit the bus. Summer vacation has officially started.

I let out another loud sigh.

Chapter 3

The bus door grinds open at the first stop, a white blocky building with a circle driveway. The sign outside the covered entry is bright green with MIDWEST JEWEL INN written across it in white paint.

Holding George's cage, Sid grins at me. "Maybe you can come see me this summer. And bring your scrapbook? I know very little about dogs and would like to learn more. If no guests are using the pool, we can go for a swim."

"Well, *maybe*. I have to help my mom in the plant shed and watch Rosie when's she gone. But if I get a free day, I'll call."

Sid's smile fades. His shoulders slump.

I get it. He doesn't think I'll call him.

"But hey, maybe you can come to *my* house. We don't have a place to swim, but we have big shade trees in the backyard so it's a cool place to hang. And bring George, we'll let him out of his cage."

"That would be stupendous." Sid is all smiles again. "I can strap George's cage on the back of my bike." A frown replaces the smile. "Of course, it depends on the pageant. I have to help my parents build a stage and set up chairs—"

Suddenly, Sid's mouth freezes in the shape of an O. Quickly, he turns to face the kids on the bus. "Our motel is hosting a contest this summer!" he yells. "A Little Princess Beauty Pageant. It is a big deal for us, so please show the slips I gave you to your parents."

He exits the bus, grinning. "I will call you later, Sammy."

"A beauty pageant? For *real*?" Rosie's face is a hundred-watt bulb. "What slip's he talking 'bout?"

Bailey pulls out her yellow slip. Yee and Anise look at theirs, too. Curious, I dig mine out of my backpack.

BE DISCOVERED! BE A STAR!
ENTER THE LITTLE PRINCESS BEAUTY PAGEANT!
WINNERS TAKE HOME CASH PRIZES AND TIARAS
TALENT SEARCH CONTEST FOR MOVIES AND MODELING
PORTRAY YOUR CULTURAL ROOTS IN THE ETHNIC BEAUTY CONTEST
SUBMIT ENTRY FORM AND ENTRY FEE BY JUNE 15
CATEGORIES INCLUDE:
Baby Miss (2–3 YRS)
Little Miss (4–5 YRS)
Pre-Junior (6–7 YRS)
Junior (8–10 YRS)
Contact Midwest Jewel Inn for information about entry fee

"June fifteenth!" Rosie's eyes turn to round saucers. The bus seat a trampoline. "But today is June first. I have to enter quick. I always wanted to be a princess."

"Not so fast, Rosie." I read the slip again. "Where you gonna get the money to enter?"

"It costs money? How much? I got five dollars and thirty-nine cents in my bank."

"Doesn't say..." Bailey pauses, reading her slip again, too. "But your mom can call and find out. And you can still be thinking about your costumes and the talent show—" Bailey starts bouncing on the seat, too. "*Ohmigosh*, I can design your costumes—just like on TV. It'll be my first professional job."

Forget the tiara....

"*Cool*," Rosie says. "And I got lots of talent. I can sing and dance, and I already have a costume. A ballerina tutu."

"That won't work." Yee looks up from her yellow slip. "At

least, not for the ethnic beauty contest. Your costume needs to portray your cultural roots."

"What's cultural roots?" Rosie twists in her seat so she's facing Yee.

"Like Chinese American. If I were going to enter, which I'm not because I'm too old, I would dress up as Fu Hao. You know, someone Chinese."

"I never heard of Hu Fao," Bailey says.

"*Fu...Hao.*" Yee's face pinches up, like she's in pain. "She was a high priestess and military general in the Shang dynasty. If I were going to enter, that's who I would go as."

"And I'm African American," Anise says. "So if I were entering, I would dress as Cleopatra."

"Cleopatra wasn't African. She was Egyptian."

"I believe Egypt's in Africa, Sammy," Bailey whispers across the aisle to me.

"Oh...yeah."

Anise claps her hands. "No, wait—I'd wear my *Igbo Mmwo* costume."

"Your *what?*" Yee's eyebrows turn into little black worms wiggling across her forehead.

"*Ig-bo Mm-wo.* It means 'maiden spirit.' They're *humongous* costumes. Bright colors and weird designs all over them. The mask hides your face so no one can tell who you are. My oldest sister had one but she didn't want it anymore so she gave it to me." Anise pauses. "But I don't wear it because it's a keepsake. Besides, I'm almost twelve—*way* too old."

"I don't have a little sister," Bailey says. "Or an older one, either. I'm an only child."

Lucky her.

"I do," Justin says, butting in again. "My little sister Patty's been taking dance since she was three. She's really good at Polish dances 'cause that's what we are." He glances at Yee and Anise, looking smug. "Wysocki's a Polish American name. I bet Mom enters her right away. She's dying for her to become a New York model."

"What's my culture, Sammy?" Rosie looks at me, eyes expectant.

"You don't have one." Our house is the next stop, so I slip into my backpack.

Rosie's eyes dissolve. Two Alka-Seltzer tablets in water.

"But if I don't have a culture," she says, "I can't be in the contest."

"Come on." Bailey leads Rosie to the bus door. "Your mom can call and get more information."

Yee tugs my sleeve and leans close. "We need to check on some things, then we'll call you."

"Yeah..." Anise glances at Justin. "When the *Jerk*'s not around."

Why are they whispering?

Bailey hears them, of course. "Call me, too." She's also whispering. "You can get me a gate pass, and I'll bike out so we can practice together. I've been *dying* to see what CountryWood's like."

Yee and Anise morph into stone statues.

"Okay?" Bailey's smile is plastic now.

Yee and Anise nod. Barely.

Though Bailey doesn't stop smiling, I know she reads the same thing in those nods that I do. She's not going to get a call from either of them.

I follow her and Rosie off the bus, take a last look at the Burbies lining the windows, and exhale slowly, relieved to be rid of them. As the bus starts up, Justin's face appears at the rear window. An *L* pressed to his forehead. His mouth, grinning ear to ear.

My face flames. My hands clench into fists.

As the bus rolls away, the tailpipe stutters *a-heh-heh-heh-heh-heh*.

Aww, man.

Like always, Max is waiting on the side of the road, imitating a pile of dead brush. Everything sticks to him like Velcro. Sticks.

Leaves. Bird feathers. Stringy hair covers his eyes, a shaggy curtain he peeks through. His nose glistens like a shiny black ball, perpetually wet. The first thing he does is stick his nose in my hand, giving it a big slurpy lick.

"Not now, Max." I push him away and wipe drool on my pant leg.

He walks over to Rosie, but she pushes him away, too. "Go 'way, Max. I've got to find Mama." She runs toward the plant shed, the pageant slip a paper butterfly fluttering in her hand.

Max migrates to Bailey, but she's hypnotized. Eyes glued on the school bus, she watches as it rounds the corner for Country-Wood and disappears in a brown dust cloud.

"We've been here longer than they have," she mumbles. "Why are *we* the outsiders?"

I figure Bailey isn't expecting me to answer, so I don't. At least she's stopped smiling. She's always Miss Happy Face with everyone else. I don't know why I'm the only one she shows that other face. The real one.

"See you tomorrow, Sammy." Bailey heads for an old white farmhouse across the road, cradling her treasure chest. A cardboard box filled with purple-and-orange plastic strings stapled to sticks.

On the way to the house, the show-and-tell begins to replay. A bad movie on rewind.

Did I *really* brag that I would make hundreds of dollars this summer? *And* buy a pedigreed puppy?

A lopsided shadow streams ahead of me, pointing the way. Mine and Max's, blended together. I had forgotten about him.

"Go away, Max. I just want to be alone." Our shadows stay linked.

Dumb old dog.

Leaving Max and his shadow on the back porch, I trudge upstairs to my bedroom, toss my backpack in the closet, and flop on the bed. Summer has finally started, but the excitement I felt this morning has faded.

Just once, couldn't something go my way?

"Samuel Smith! Get down here this minute!" Mom's voice is loud. So loud, I can hear it all the way from the plant shed.

And she called me Samuel.

Great, just great. What've I done now?

Chapter 4

"How could you tell Rosie she was uncultured?" Mom is wearing her furious face. A traffic light blinking chili-pepper red. "Are you ashamed of us? Is that it? Why? Because we live in an old house instead of a...a warehouse with cement floors and granite countertops? I'll have you know this house has an upstanding history. It was built the same year Lincoln freed the slaves. Why, it could be on the historic register...if we had the money to restore it."

"I didn't mean it like that, Mom. I like our house. It's cool. Not because of that historic stuff. Because it belonged to Grandpa before we moved in."

Our house is made of limestone blocks. Settlers who came to the Midwest dug quarries in the hillsides and chiseled building stones out of huge chunks of limestone. A lot of the houses they built are still lived in. Like ours.

"Then why?" Mom's faded blond hair is tied on her neck. Her chambray shirt is dirt-stained. Her jeans are grubby at the knees. "It's because I do this kind of work, isn't it?" She holds out her hands, studying fingernails worn to nubs.

Mom's sore spot is showing. Someone has made her feel like they're better than she is. When she's really tired, she talks to herself. Saying things like *What's so important about Bluetooth technology?* And *When did a secretary become an executive assistant?* And *So what if I don't know how to play Mah-jongg?* Mom didn't go past high school, but that didn't matter until Dad died. She's determined that Rosie and I go to college. Like Beth.

"Not that, either." I tell her about the bus ride home, replay the talk about cultures, and watch the traffic light blink from red to normal: suntanned and weathered. "Read the slip, Mom."

Her face blinks red again, from embarrassment this time. She turns to Rosie and wipes tears off her freckled cheeks. "I didn't understand, Rosie. You see, everyone has a culture, ours is just mixed up. We have a little bit of a lot of things in us. That's the way it is for people who've been in this country a long time."

Rosie's eyes light up. "So I can dress up as anything I want?"

Mom nods.

"Then I want to be an Igloo Mojo. I just know Anise will loan me her costume."

I groan and tell Mom about Anise's *Igbo Mmwo* costume and Yee's talk about Chinese warrior priestesses.

"Maybe I spoke too soon." Mom's eyes blink slowly. "Some things we're not. Chinese or African, for example. But we are part Scottish. And *Indian,* too."

"We're Indian like Sid?"

I let out a bigger groan and explain that Sid is from the *country* of India.

"No, not that kind of Indian." Mom blows out her breath, looking tired. "I don't have any proof of it, but your grandpa told me once we were part Chippewa. A great-great-grandmother, I think."

I envision a pink feather headdress, green sequins on fake buckskin, and tell Mom that Bailey wants to design Rosie's costumes. "But since we can't *prove* we're Indian, maybe Rosie should dress up as someone from Scotland."

"Oh, Scottish would definitely be best," Mom says. She's seen Bailey's original Barbie doll clothes, too.

"What would that look like?" Rosie looks between Mom and me.

I turn to a statue, knowing when to keep my mouth shut.

"Well, I know the Scots wore kilts...."

"Kilts? They wore dead things?"

"A kilt is a skirt. The Scots wear beautiful plaid skirts and matching shawls over their shoulders. Your grandma could make you one easy." Mom hesitates, eyes blinking. "But I'm not sure she's up to it. Her memory's slipping so fast, worse every day."

I like the idea of my grandma making Rosie's costume, but she moves like a snail now and doesn't remember things the way she used to. It's like an invisible curtain is closing in front of her, the opening getting narrower and narrower with every tick of the clock.

"Yeah, and I'll rig up a fake bagpipe for the talent part." I squeeze a make-believe bagpipe under my arm and spew screeching noises out of my mouth.

Rosie scowls at me, not amused. "I'm going as a Chippy-wa and do an Indian dance. And Bailey will make me an Indian princess dress with sequins all over it."

Another groan slips out of my mouth. Mom gets the message.

"Slow down, Rosie. I'm not positive we *are* Chippewa. I mean, we don't have proof."

"Grandpa wouldn't lie."

Mom's shoulders droop, a sign she's giving up. "Who's to know we can't prove it?" She sighs, looking at me.

I give up, too. Why should I be the only Smith to look like a fool?

But when Rosie starts stomping in a circle and grunting like a caveman, I start to waffle. Justin's sister has been taking dance since she was three years old, and her parents can buy her fancy costumes because they're rich. Rosie *will* look like a fool if Bailey makes her costume, especially if she dances like Bigfoot. But how can I stop her?

The same way you were stopped, says a voice in my head.

"Wait, Mom—it costs money to enter the contest."

"Money? How much?"

"Don't know. There's a phone number on the slip."

Mom looks at the yellow slip. "I'll call right way. Opportunities like this don't come along every day, and Rosie's been dreaming about something like this for a long time." She pauses, looking at me. "Oh, and the sign out front needs touching up, Sammy. First thing tomorrow morning?"

"Mom, summer just started—"

"Which is the busiest time of the year in my business. Plenty of time to rest come winter."

"I'm in school all winter."

"I'm not going to argue with you, Sammy."

"Okay, okay. I'll paint the sign tomorrow morning."

"Good. And raccoons paid us a visit last night. They broke flowerpots and dug up the compost pile. Looked like four sets of tracks. I figure a mother and three kits."

That explains the smell of compost everywhere. Dried leaves. Sphagnum moss. Earthworms.

"So you know what that means." Mom grins at me. "Add another job to your list."

"Aww, Mom." I speak up before she can bust my chops again. "Okay, I'll clean up after the raccoons, too."

She gives me a quick hug. Turning for the house, she pushes aside a big shaggy lump. "Not now, Max. I need to call the hotel. Hopefully I don't have to break someone's heart."

Oh, sure! Wouldn't do for someone in our family to have a broken heart.

Max noses my hand, his mouth a leaking faucet. "Go find someone else to pester, Max. I told you, I just want to be alone."

Chapter 5

Saturday. The first morning of summer break. I open my eyes and stare at lint buildup on the blades of the ceiling fan. We have fans in every room and keep the windows open for a cross-breeze in the summer. Sunlight dapples the walls and dust motes swim in the air. Lots of big trees keep the house shady except in the winter, which works well because the sun warms the house up fast after the leaves fall.

I watch the fan spinning…spinning…slightly off center so one blade complains when it reaches the high spot.

Sgreak.

I look at the clock—almost seven—close my eyes again. I sleep late in the summer, get up around seven-thirty…

Sgreak.

Usually.

Sighing, I swing my legs over the side of the bed and change sleeping shorts and tee for daytime shorts and tee. Reeboks. No socks.

Mom's already in the garden shed, getting an order ready for a customer in town to pick up. I know because she told us her schedule last night at supper. After that, she's doing a garden plan for someone at CountryWood. Which means the rest of us are on our own for breakfast. But we learned to fend for ourselves a long time ago. Mom's never been much of a housekeeper or cook. Plants are her specialty.

Downstairs, Beth stands at the kitchen counter. Faded jeans, cotton shirt tied at her waist, blond hair in a ponytail. She's fixing a breakfast sandwich, cream cheese on a whole-wheat bagel, which she'll eat as she drives to the animal hospital. After that, she'll go to the shelter. Both jobs are important since she wants to become a vet.

"Don't forget to feed the cats," she tells Rosie on her way out the door. She pauses, looking at me. "And Max."

"I know, I know!" I don't know which is worse. A bossy older sister or a little one who cries to get her way. "I've been feeding him for four years now. You know, the dog who was supposed to be on his last legs?"

"Who knew he was immortal?" The back screen slams and Beth's old Subaru chokes to life, wheezing down the driveway.

That word again. *Immortal.* But I know Beth was just joking around. We've all learned that nothing lives forever. All at once, I think of my dad, who I never really knew, my grandpa, who I did, and feel empty inside.

Rosie comes in, wearing denim shorts, pink tee, and sandals. She gets out a box of cereal and a carton of milk and fills a bowl. Cats start showing up in twos and threes at the screen door, then the entire back porch is full. All of them screeching.

"Geez, Rosie. Feed them quick so they'll shut up."

"Have to rinse out my bowl first." On the way to the sink, she dribbles milk across the linoleum. Twenty-eight clawed feet attack the screen door, trying to get to the spill.

"Just *go.* I'll clean up."

Rosie turns into a pigtailed Pied Piper, toting a bag of Cat Chow as she leads the horde to their food dishes. To me, they're just cats. But to Rosie, they're her children.

"You'll be Sunday," she tells the white one, sounding like a schoolteacher giving an assignment. "And you're Monday...." Her voice fades as she moves away from the house.

Finally, the kitchen is quiet. I clean up the spill, put a frozen waffle in the toaster, and stare at poster board squares on the table. Rosie spent last evening making birth certificates for her cats. On each square is a picture of a cat, tail sticking straight up, and underneath, a printed description. *White with black spots. Black with white spots. Gray tiger. Orange tiger. Calico. Siamese blue. Black.* Spotting her box of crayons on the table, I figure the pictures will be colored in before lunch.

I spread grape jelly on my waffle and look over the stack of certificates as I eat. In the *Name* spot are different days of the week, but the vital statistics all read the same.

Date of Birth: Unknown
Sex: Neutered
Place of Birth: U.S.A.
Parents' names: Mama Cat and Daddy Cat

I can tell Beth helped Rosie with the certificates because the wording sounds official. There's even a drawing that looks like a government seal in the bottom corner, complete with what's supposed to be an American eagle.

Pushing Rosie's birth certificates aside, I pick up the morning paper where Mom left it. Before I know it, I'm reading the section on *Pets and Supplies* in the want ads.

```
Basset Hound Puppies. Registered, 1st shots
and dewormed, 3 males, 1 female, $450 each.
```

The first ad is an eye-opener. Justin was right, purebred dogs *do* cost a lot of money. I read on.

```
Boston Terrier Pups AKC. 2 black & white
males, $475, 6 weeks old. 1 black & white
female, $525, 8 weeks old. Dewclaws removed,
shots and wormed. Ready to go.
```

I can't believe it. The cost is going up. Geez, have I been living in a cave?

One ad is of real interest. For Sid, though, not me.

```
Chihuahua Puppies. Two male Chihuahuas.
Asking $550. They are CKC registered and have
their first puppy shots.
```

Sid wants a Chihuahua, but if he could only afford $9.98 at PetSmart for George, he'll never get one. I look at the listing again, wonder what CKC stands for. AKC stands for American Kennel Club. Maybe Chihuahua Kennel Club? Could this tiny little dog have its own club? It's the only thing that makes sense. I move to another ad.

```
Cavalier King Charles Spaniels. 2 male
Cavaliers for sale. 1 tan and a little white.
One tricolor. $850. Get ahold of me for
pictures.
```

"Aww, man. They're getting higher."

```
English Bulldog Puppies. 11 weeks old.
1 male, 1 female. AKC Grand Champion parents.
Shots, microchip, and health check. Buy
quality puppies from a show home. $1,500.
```

"Fifteen hundred dollars—that can't be right." I read the ad again. Not a mistake. The puppies cost fifteen...hundred... dollars. *Each.*

Only halfway through the ads and my stomach is churning. Realizing the listings are alphabetical, I skip down the page. Drumbeats pound my chest when I find the listing.

```
German Shepherd Pups. AKC Registered. 8 weeks
old. 1st shots. 3 males and one female $350.
```

The ad includes the picture of a puppy just like the one I want. A sable German shepherd. Three hundred fifty dollars is a fortune, but compared to the rest, it's a bargain.

I skip over ads for other dogs—Min Pin/Chi-Weenie mix pups, poodle-Bichons, and Shih-poos—all of which cost from $300 up. Even crossbred puppies cost more than I've saved up.

Suddenly, an idea slips into my head. What if I *could* earn enough money to buy one of the German shepherd puppies?

"Yeah, right."

I toss the paper in the trash can, slam the back door, and trudge to the plant shed. Outside, someone yells my name. Underneath a big shade tree across the road, purple-and-orange pom-poms wave at me. Bailey is practicing cheerleading. Alone.

The sign in front of our place says:

Smith's Flower Shed
Specializing in Annual & Perennial Plants
& Garden Designs
Will Plant Your Garden for You

Hours of business and our phone number follow. Before Mom left this morning, she wrote out instructions for the sign to make sure I got it right. Jars of paint—red, yellow, and blue—sit on the counter.

I like working in the shed. The musty-earth smell. Rust-colored clay pots. Living rainbows of geraniums and petunias. And it's quiet. Most of the time, there aren't any people. Just butterflies and bees buzzing around and sucking up nectar.

Rosie walks in as I put the final touches on the sign.

"What does that mean?" She points to the line that reads M-TU-W-F: 9:00 AM – 5:00 PM.

"That stands for Monday, Tuesday, Wednesday, and Friday, from nine in the morning until five in the afternoon."

"And that?" She points to the line that reads TH: 9:00 AM – 9:00 PM.

"*TH* stands for Thursday. Mom stays open late that night."

"*Oh*, I get it. It's the first *two* letters of the word."

"Right. Some days of the week start with the same letter. Like Tuesday and Thursday."

"So *that* means Saturday?"

I look where she's pointing. "Yeah, *SA* stands for Saturday. We're open from nine in the morning until eight at night on Saturday. You know, for people who work during the week."

She frowns. "Then what does *that* mean?" She points to the line that reads SN: 1 PM – 4 PM.

"Sunday from one o'clock until four o'clock. Lot of people go to church on Sunday mornings, so Mom doesn't open up until later."

She frowns again. "But that's not right."

I look at what I've painted, check it against Mom's note. "Is too. See?" I show her the note. "It says 1 PM to 4 PM."

"Not *that*. It should be SU, not *SN*. *Sunday* is spelled S-U-N-D—"

"I know how to spell *Sunday*, Rosie."

"Then why did you put *SN*? It should be *SU*. Like *TH* for *Thursday* and *SA* for *Saturday*. Why's it different?"

I stare at the abbreviation. "Don't know. Ask Mom or Beth."

"I thought you were smart, Sammy."

Suddenly, I'm jealous of Bailey. Why couldn't I have been an only child?

Rosie picks up a small paintbrush. "Can I have some paint, please?"

"What do you need paint for?"

"To paint my cats."

I remember the birth certificates on the kitchen table. "I guess, but don't use too much. Mom might want me to paint something else. And wash the brush out when you're done."

"You're being bossy, Sammy." She picks up the box of paints and heads toward the house.

"Learn to live with it, runt!" I yell. "After Beth leaves, I'm next boss in line."

"I'm gonna tell Mom!" Rosie yells over her shoulder.

Great. She will, too. I decide it's time to clean up after the raccoons.

A raccoon can make a big mess. A mother raccoon and three babies, a humongous mess. After cleaning out the leftover dirt, I wash the clay pots and set them in the sun to dry. Clay takes a long time, a lot longer than plastic. But the thermometer on the wall reads ninety degrees, so they should be dry by the time Mom gets home.

It's almost lunchtime when the black cat walks in front of me, a big yellow *F* painted on its side.

"Rosie..."

Chapter 6

"Samuel Smith—why did you tell Rosie it was okay to paint the cats?" Mom paces the shed, hands gripping her hips like they're holding up her jeans.

Beth is home, too, looking at jars of paint that I rescued from Rosie after I discovered the painted cats. The black one wasn't the only one with a letter on it. Every one of them now has the abbreviation for a day of the week painted on its side or between its ears.

"I didn't. I mean, I thought she was going to use the paint on birth certificates."

"How could you make a mistake like that?"

"Me? Rosie's the one who screwed up. Where is she, anyway? You should be busting her chops, not mine."

"Upstairs. I stopped by to talk to your grandmother about costumes. We drew some sketches for Rosie to look at."

My grandma lives in an assisted living place. My grandpa lived there, too, before he died. I never knew my dad's parents. They lived in Florida and didn't like to travel. I don't miss them because I never knew them. But I really miss Grandpa. He taught me all kinds of things. How to patch a bike inner tube. Change a tire on the car. Use a toothpick to fix a loose screw on a cabinet door. Stuff steel wool in holes to keep mice out of the garage.

"So Grandma's making Rosie's costumes?" I smile at Mom, hoping to get her talking about the pageant so she'll forget about cats.

"No, your grandmother's not up to the job. But maybe with

her help, I can manage a couple...if they're not too elaborate."
She shakes her head, glancing across the road. "You were right,
Sammy. Bailey's just not the right person."

An image of Bailey pops into my head. Practicing cheerleading. Alone. She'll be totally flattened if she can't make Rosie's
costumes, and it will be my fault.

"Are you *really* going through with this pageant thing, Mom?
I mean, how much does it cost, anyway?"

"Yes, I'm going through with it. Rosie has her heart set on
it and..." Mom rubs the back of her neck, looking tired. "The
entry fee is one hundred and fifty dollars—but it's a rare opportunity, one that may not come around again."

"One hundred and fifty dollars!"

"Now, back to this cat business," Mom says. "Tell me what
happened."

"Don't remember." I'm burning. I can't believe Mom is giving
Rosie a hundred fifty dollars for a beauty pageant. *And* paying
for costumes.

Beth looks up from the paint label she's been reading. "Come
on, Spammy, it's important. What exactly did Rosie say?"

"Don't call me *that*. If you have to talk to me, call me by my
real name."

Beth stares at me, eyes wide. "Geez, chill out, little bro. Now,
what *exactly* did Rosie say...*Samuel Allen Smith*?" She grins,
dimples showing.

I can't help grinning, too. Beth is cool. And pretty. Hazel
eyes. Wavy blond hair, which she leaves natural. No dyed pastel
streaks. No metal in her nose or navel, either. She'd rather have
a 4.0 grade-point average. And the guys she dates aren't greasy
creeps. They have swag. Hair clean. Shirts ironed. Pants belted.
And they don't talk down to you.

"Sam is okay. Or Sammy. Just not *Spammy*." I cool down
and take a deep breath, trying to sort things out. "Well, see, I
asked Rosie what she needed paint for and she said for her cats.
She was making birth certificates at the kitchen table and I just

figured..." Gravitational pull takes over, dragging my shoulders downward. "She said 'please.'"

"You simply must do better." Mom's hands are still holding up her jeans. "You have to listen to what people are saying."

"Wh-what? That's all I do, Mom. Listen to what people tell me."

"I mean *really* saying. You know, read between the lines."

"Wait up. How can you read between the lines of words people are saying?"

"Don't be a smart-mouth, Sam. You know what I mean."

I read between the lines. I'm supposed to be a mind reader.

"Chill, Mom. He's twelve years old."

"I know, I know." Mom wags her head, sighing. "I'm sorry, Sam. I just need to trust that you're going to watch out for your little sister when I'm gone."

"I *do*, Mom."

"Ask more questions to make sure you understand what she's saying. *Exactly* what she's saying."

"Okay, more questions."

"The paint's nontoxic, so no harm done." Beth grins again. "When I asked why she did it, Rosie said it was so she could remember their new names. You have to admit, it was a clever idea."

"Yeah, clever idea, Mom. And the paint won't hurt them."

Mom sighs again. "All right...this time." She waves a finger in front of my nose. "But next time—"

"I'll ask lots of questions."

"Good. Now, let's go have lunch. I'm bushed. My customer this morning was picky. Had to move some of the plants three times."

The garden shed where Mom sells plants is on the side of the road and has a gravel drive where customers can park. A gate leading to our backyard separates the business from the house. If customers come while we're inside, they can ring a big dinner bell outside the shed to get our attention.

"At least you and Rosie remembered to water the animals." Beth checks the dishes on the screened back porch. A pet door allows Max and the cats to come and go at will.

But I did forget.

I look at Max's water dish. Still full, but cloudy. Bugs floating.

Beth leans closer, inspecting the food dishes. First the cats'. Then Max's. When she's done with Max's, she looks at me. Eyes not blinking. Brows reaching for the sky.

I look, too. See Dog Chow, greasy from heat. More bugs. A stream of ants.

I think back to when Beth brought Max home, how he wouldn't eat or drink unless I brought it to him. Mom figured he probably belonged to a kid my age and I reminded Max of him. Like it or not, next thing I know, I'm the one training him. Brushing him. Picking up after him. Feeding him.

So why isn't he eating now?

I follow Mom into the kitchen to help with lunch. She's just calmed down, and I want her to stay that way.

Beth takes sandwich makings and a pitcher of iced tea from the refrigerator. I retrieve plates and glasses from the cupboard. Mom checks the answering machine. Finding the light blinking, she hits the Listen button.

Call us, Sammy. Yee's voice booms out of the answering machine. *Soon as you can.*

Yeah. Anise's voice this time. *It's important.*

Mom and Beth look at me.

"They're friends from school. I'll, uh, I'll call from the living room."

"You *are* growing up, little bro," Beth says, grinning. "Two girls at a time?"

"It's not like that."

Mom smiles, too.

I give up. Let them think what they want.

"I'm going to do *what*?"

I'm at Mom's desk in the living room, which looks onto the

county road. Anise is at Yee's house. They're talking on the speakerphone in her dad's office. Both are so excited, I have to listen hard to understand what they're saying.

"We talked to someone who works at the CountryWood office," Anise says. "The woman who does the newsletter. She works part-time—on Monday, Wednesday, and Friday—and she sounded *real* interested when we told her our idea. See, she'd like someone to walk her dog on the days she's working 'cause she can't."

"So it's all decided," Yee says.

"*What?* Who decided *what?*" I watch a car approach, but it doesn't stop at our place.

Like a lot of old houses, ours sits close to the county road. The rooms are small with high ceilings and old-fashioned woodwork, except the kitchen and bathrooms. Grandpa remodeled those when rusty pipes turned the water orange. Things that wouldn't fit in Grandpa and Grandma's retirement apartment mingle with things Mom and Dad owned. Grandma's knitted afghans hug furniture. Dad's John Grisham paperbacks stuff bookshelves. Grandpa's can of Prince Albert tobacco perfumes the house. Mom's ivy droops from tall things; floor plants reach for the ceiling. And squeezed among all of it are bits and pieces of Beth, Rosie, and me. Outside, the house is plain beige rock; inside, a Goodwill store.

Something else outside the window gets my attention. Bailey, sitting on her front porch.

"Me and Yee," Anise says. "We decided."

"Yee and I," Yee tells Anise. "That's the correct way to say it."

"Yee and I," Anise repeats. "You're going to run an ad in the newsletter to find people who want their dogs walked on Monday, Wednesday, and Friday. An ad costs ten dollars up to fifteen words, and twenty cents a word after that. Oh, and you have to pay with cash, a money order, or a check."

Ten dollars! I only have a hundred saved…but I could make a lot more if I got enough customers.

"And the deadline's Monday," Yee says. "So you need to get

your ad to her that morning. Oh, and bring your credentials so you can show her how much you know."

"Credentials?"

"Your dog book." Yee lets out a long sigh that says *Catch up, Slug Boy.*

"How much will she pay me for walking her dog?"

Silence. Then Yee says, "You'll have to negotiate that yourself. Do you expect us to do everything?"

Translation: They forgot to ask.

"And you have to talk to Chief Beaumont, the head of security," Anise says. "But he lives across the street from us so there won't be a problem. He said he could issue you a special pass for the days of the week you'll be coming out, but he needs to explain the rules to you."

"There's rules for walking dogs?"

"*Of course.*" Yee's using her matter-of-fact tone. Miss Know-it-all. "What time Monday can you be here?"

"Uh, better call you back." I glance toward the kitchen, where Mom and Beth are still discussing painted cats. "Need to talk to my mom first."

"Well, hurry up," Anise says. "Chief Beaumont's expecting you Monday. *Early.* We're supposed to let him know so he can get you on his calendar."

"Call you right back."

Back in the kitchen, Mom and Beth stare at me. I look between them, searching for the right words to tell them about my new job.

Tactful, the voice in my head says. *Be tactful.*

"I got a job!" Words gush out like water over a broken dam. "I'm gonna walk dogs for people at CountryWood three days a week. Mondays, Wednesdays, and Fridays."

Mom stares at me, mouth hanging open.

"*Wow,* that's cool." Beth gives me a knuckle bump.

Mom closes her mouth and glares at Beth. "What do you mean, *cool*? Now that you're working full-time and leaving home in August, I need him here."

"Mom, I really want to do this—I *need* to do this. It's...it's important."

"You just can't, Sammy. It won't work."

"Sure it will," Beth says. "You said the same thing when I got a job, remember? All we have to do is work out a schedule. I can move things around so I'm working alternate times from Sammy." She looks at Mom, eyes serious. "Sammy's growing up, needs some independence."

Mom's face softens. "Well, if you're willing to do that." She looks at me, sighing. "What's so important that you had to get a job?"

"It's a...surprise."

Mom's forehead creases. "I don't like surprises."

I rub my mouth, a lot. Pace the kitchen, a lot. Sigh deep, a lot.

"Sammy—"

"To buy a purebred puppy." I spit out the words and watch Mom's mouth drop open again.

"*Puppy*—" Beth makes a thick *gluck* sound. "You can get all kinds of puppies at the shelter for *nothing*. Hundreds of dogs are just begging to be adopted."

"It's not the same. I want a dog of my own, one I pick out myself. You know, like in my dog book."

"*Oh,* your dog book." Mom pauses, looking at Beth. "He's been dreaming about this for a long time. And remember, you're the one who got him started on that dog book."

"Yeah, but..." Beth's shoulders slump, a sign she's caving.

"No, wait." Mom's forehead furrows with lines again. "It just won't work, Sammy. You know what we talked about. It would be too hard on old Max. A puppy would run him ragged—and us. Remember how it was when Max came to live with us? He just about destroyed the place."

"Yeah, but that was different," Beth says. "Max was never trained and had been mistreated. It was Sammy who changed that. He spent hours working with him."

"Yeah, Mom." I send Beth a thank-you look. "And I'll train the puppy from the start so it won't be a problem."

"I say he should go for it," Beth says.

I decide seventeen-year-old sisters are great. They understand things because they've been through them already. Little sisters with big ears are another thing.

"How much they gonna pay you?" Rosie peeks around the door frame.

"Uh, don't know yet. Have to negotiate salary when I meet with them."

"Them people are dumb rich."

"It's *those* people," Mom says. "And who told you that?"

"Beth. She says they burn money."

Mom gives Beth a raised-eyebrow look.

"Well, they do, Mom," Beth says. "I deal with them at the clinic all the time. They're *so* obnoxious. I mean, money means nothing to them. It runs through their fingers like water." She pauses, looking at me. "But maybe that's a good thing because that means they'll pay better than people like us could."

"People like us?" Mom's eyebrows reach for the sky.

Beth shrugs. "Let's face it, we're not exactly rolling in dough." She glances around our kitchen. "You've been inside the castle walls out there, so you know what I'm talking about."

Mom looks around the kitchen, too. "Well, what you say may be true, but not *all* the people at CountryWood are 'rolling in dough.' Some of my customers live quite modestly. I really don't think Sammy will make enough money to buy a pedigreed dog, but..." She looks at me and sighs. "Okay, you can do this. But if you do get a puppy and it annoys Max, it will have to go. Agreed?"

"Yeah, okay. Thanks, Mom."

"And trust me," she says, "you're lucky to be living where you do. Our place is a lot nicer than anything I've seen out there. Prettier, too." She fills glasses with iced tea. "Now, let's eat."

"Well, I still think *those* people have money to burn," Beth whispers, leaning close. "So start high when you set your salary."

I think of Justin. His four-hundred-dollar dog. Twenty-five-hundred-dollar golf cart. I say, "Yeah, some people get all the luck."

"Yeah." The smile slides off Beth's face.

I know what Beth is thinking. She got into a good school in Colorado and has been working hard to save money for books and expenses. Studying hard, too, so she could get a partial scholarship and a work-study program. Going to that school is the most important thing in life to her.

"Wait up." Mom sticks out her hand like a big-city traffic cop.

Oh, no, she's changing her mind. . . .

"You can't let your chores slide."

Breath I didn't know I was holding explodes from my mouth. "Sure, of course, no problem, I'll take care of everything. I'll feed Max right now and mow the front yard soon as it cools off some."

I hurry to the back door and stop, looking at Mom. "Oh . . . and Bailey should be the one to make Rosie's costumes. She keeps up with pageants on TV and knows the latest styles and . . . and just because she should."

"Yeah, I want Bailey, too," Rosie says. "I didn't like the pictures you and Grandma drew."

Mom looks at Beth.

"I say give the girl a chance," Beth says. "She's been dreaming about being a designer since she could walk."

"Well, maybe." Mom sighs. "Your granny seems to be slipping faster every day."

I leave Rosie doing her version of a pirouette and hurry outside. Noticing that Max's food and water dish still haven't been touched, I try to remember when I saw him last.

Friday. Friday after school.

Then I remember the last thing I told him: *I just want to be alone.*

I look across the backyard, which is at least two acres, maybe more. It was part of a farm when Grandpa owned it. He sold off most of the land, but after Dad died, Grandpa deeded Mom the part where the house, the garage, and the garden shed sit, plus the space where Mom grows perennials. Black walnut and oak trees grow out back, wild raspberries and native honeysuckle. A haven for squirrels, possums, raccoons. And occasionally, foxes.

Mom was happy to get the place because it meant no mortgage payments. Just taxes, utilities, and repairs. Which cost plenty. Beth, Rosie, and I love living there. Plenty of space to do our thing. Tree house. Sandbox. Horseshoe pit. Basketball hoop. Max loved it, too. Right away, he became territorial, keeping animals away from the house. Stray dogs. Possums. Raccoons. Squirrels—especially squirrels, which bury walnuts and acorns all over. The ground looks like miniature land mines have detonated everywhere. Brown eruptions on a field of green.

That's it. He's treed a squirrel and won't let it come to ground....

Dumping Max's dog bowls, I refill them—fresh Dog Chow in one, cold water from the yard spigot in the other—and make a mad dash back inside.

I have important business to take care of. First, call Yee and Anise to confirm my job interview with the head of security and then write an ad to take to the woman who does the Country-Wood newsletter. And since she could be my first customer, I need to find out what kind of dog she has so I can study my dog book.

It hits me then. Monday's become a school day and a big test is scheduled. The biggest exam of my life. If I don't do well, she may not hire me.

Suddenly, a land mine erupts in my stomach.

Chapter 7

"So, your appointment's tomorrow morning?"

Beth is fixing a spinach and tomato salad for Sunday-night supper. I'm spreading egg salad on pumpernickel bread. Mom's in the garden, potting perennials, and Rosie's feeding the days of the week.

"Yep. Nine o'clock sharp."

"Nervous?"

"*Nah.* My friends are meeting me at the front gate. They'll introduce me to everyone. Did you find something on peekapoos like I asked? Everything I've collected is on purebred dogs, not mixed."

Beth points to a printout of a web page on the table. "One of the dogs is a peekapoo?"

"*Two* peekapoos." Yee and Anise gave me the news when I confirmed my appointment last night. "Part Pekingese and part poodle. I'm kinda surprised those people out there would have a mutt."

"I wouldn't call them *mutts* in front of the owner. Lot of dogs today are deliberately crossbred to achieve certain traits. They're called designer breeds."

I stare at Beth. "For real?"

"Yeah, for real—"

"Help! Help!" Rosie slams through the back door, eyes streaming.

"What is it?" Beth grabs her. "Are you hurt?"

"It's Max—he's going to kill Monday and Thursday."

Beth and I run for the door. Rosie follows. Mom sees us race past and chases after us. We find Max standing next to an overgrown evergreen bush behind the barn. Two of Rosie's cats are nearby, pacing.

"Wait. There's something in the branches." Beth moves closer to investigate. "I think that's what the cats are interested in."

Max inserts himself between Beth and the bush.

"Watch out." Mom arrives, breathless. "He could be sick. One of my customers told me last week about a stray dog that had distemper."

"What's distemper?" Rosie's face is streaked with tears and dirt.

"A viral disease that affects dogs."

Rosie starts to wail again. "Are my cats gonna get sick, too?"

"None of our animals are going to get sick, Rosie. They've had their shots." Beth watches Max awhile, then laughs. "He's found a nest, a robin's nest. And a bird's sitting on it."

Mom moves up next to Beth. "You don't think Max is protecting it?"

"That's exactly what I think. The nesting site's low to the ground, too low to be safe. Could be a first-time mama who miscalculated a good building site."

"Wonder where the male bird is?" Mom scans the treetops, then looks at Beth. "Robins are monogamous, aren't they?"

"Usually."

"What's that mean?" Rosie walks closer, too.

"It means a bird stays with one mate for the breeding season."

I look up at the trees, see blue jays, finches, and blackbirds. Chattering because we're trespassing in their space. No male robin.

Sunday and Wednesday join Monday and Thursday. Almost a full week of cats, walking back and forth. Tails lashing.

"My bet is the male bird disappeared for some reason," Beth says. "Some animal could have gotten him. Maybe one of the cats."

Rosie's eyes overflow again. "My cats aren't bird killers."

Beth squats on her heels so she can look Rosie in the eye. "All cats are bird killers. It's normal. That's probably why Max chased them away. He wasn't trying to kill Monday and Thursday. He was protecting Birdie." She stands up, staring at Max. "*That's* the odd part."

"It *is* strange." Mom looks at Beth. "Why do you suppose Max took it in his head to do it? Have you ever heard of something like this before?"

Beth shakes her head, then looks at me. "You noticed anything different about Max lately? You're around him more than anyone else."

"Me? No, nothing."

But I did tell him to pester someone else....

"Well, he must have stumbled on her by accident and decided she needed help."

"There could be other reasons, too." Beth's forehead wrinkles up, like she's thinking about something. "Maybe the male bird *did* mate with more than one female. If he changed partners for a second brood, he's probably taking care of the other family. He can only pull so many worms out of the ground, you know."

"And then Max fell in love with Birdie." Rosie is all smiles. "So they're married now."

I stare at my little sister, dumbfounded. "Dogs don't fall in love with birds, stupid."

"Don't call your sister names, Sammy."

"But he's right." Beth pulls Rosie close. "Dogs and birds don't fall in love like that. Max just adopted the new family."

"*Oh.*" Rosie gets real bouncy. "Maybe some new daddy will adopt us, too."

Making a choking sound, Mom hurries toward the garden shed. "I have some work to finish up," she says over her shoulder. Voice tight. Strained.

After Dad's accident, Mom went into a deep depression, hardly talking at all. Which is why we don't mention him much. It's like a knife twisting in her gut.

"Geez, where do you get this stuff, Rosie? That is so ... *dumb.*"

"Ease off, Sammy." Beth leads Rosie away from the nest. "Go help Mom, tell her supper's almost ready."

Rosie calls the cats to follow her. Once they're gone, Max curls up in the grass near the nest.

"If that's not proof," Beth says, "I don't know what is."

"Dumb old dog."

"Pretty smart, I'd say." Beth looks at me, eyes serious. "Max's food and water dish are dirty again. Freshen both of them and bring them down here. He's not going to leave that nest."

"What? No way! Rosie's the one who upset Mom, not me. Let her do it, I have a job now."

"What's wrong with you, Sammy?" Beth's eyebrows scrunch up. "Your attitude sucks lately."

Because nothing's fair! Why can't anyone see that?

"Remember, Rosie's only six. She'd just been born when the accident happened, so she has no memories of Dad." She pauses, shaking her head slightly. "It's hard to miss someone you never knew."

"Well, I don't remember him much, either. And you're the one who brought Max home, so *you* haul stuff back here."

"We tried that, remember? He only responded to you. Not me. Not Mom. Nobody except *you*. And you've done a great job with him all these years." She pauses. "Besides, I'm handling two jobs as it is. And remember, I'm rearranging my schedule so you can work, too."

"Yeah, well…it still sucks."

Her eyes narrow to slits. "Look, if you don't take care of Max properly, I'll tell Mom and she won't let you take that job." She walks toward the house, talking over her shoulder. "Twice a day—*fresh* food and water twice a day."

"That's blackmail."

"Yep. And that bird could use some water, too. Grab that old birdbath out of the shed." She stops, looking at the wild raspberry bushes next to Mom's garden. "She's close to food, plenty of earthworms in the grass, but she needs water."

"I have to babysit a dog—and a bird?" I look at the robin, sitting in a mud-and-stick nest inside a fortress of evergreen branches. "How long does it take to hatch eggs?"

"Couple of weeks, but we don't know when she started sitting. Could be shorter. Maybe a week?"

"Oh. Well, a week's not too bad."

"After that, she'll take care of the hatchlings another couple weeks until they're strong enough to fly. Fend for themselves."

"Two to three weeks? No way Max will hang around *that* long."

"I'll take that bet." Beth grins. "And shake it! Supper will be on the table in five minutes."

Beth disappears, leaving me with Max. He thumps his tail on the ground and gives me a shaggy grin. His breath smells like squashed bugs. Bittersweet, like sauerkraut. Since he hasn't been to the house, I decide he probably did eat some. Hot-weather insects are thick. Grasshoppers in the grass. Cicadas buzzing through trees. June bugs chewing on bushes. He'll eat anything.

On the long trudge to the back porch, I wonder how a day that started out so good could end up so bad. Just as I got a job that would fix everything, Max had to adopt a bird. Which means I now have *two* new jobs. Since there's no water spigot at the barn, I'll have to bucket water twice a day—for a dog and a bird—and haul down Dog Chow.

I feel like wringing Max's neck.

Rosie's, too.

And Beth's—*especially* Beth's.

It's a conspiracy.

"Sammy, are you still up?" Mom calls from the bottom of the stairs. "What are you doing? It's getting late."

The clock on my nightstand says 10:06. "Working on something. I'll be done in a minute."

"Working on something...like what?"

"You know, getting ready for tomorrow. I have to go to CountryWood in the morning."

"Well, don't stay up too much longer."

"Almost done."

I go back to working on my ad for the CountryWood

newsletter. I've been studying ads in the *Services/Businesses* section of the want ads, trying to figure out the important things to say. Like, the job I'm looking for. And why I'd be good to hire. And how much I charge. And how to contact me.

I read what I've written.

Do you need someone to walk your dog? Hire me! I'm full of energy. Have tons of experience and credentials. And I will pick up your dog's poop. Call Samuel Allen Smith at...

I pause, wondering if phone numbers count as words. If I count the number as one word, I have thirty-four words. If two, thirty-five. I decide it counts as one, but it's still too many. And I haven't mentioned cost yet.

I study the want ads in the paper some more. A few minutes later, I rewrite my ad and count the words again.

Rent a dog walker. Experienced. Can provide credentials. Will pick up and dispose of dog poop. Fair rates but you need to pay in cash every day. Call Sammy Smith at...

"Aw, man. Thirty-two words!"

I notice none of the ads in the newspaper mention names and decide not to mention mine. Fifteen minutes later, I've worn out the eraser on my pencil, but the ad includes all the really important things. Now, if only it's short enough.

Will walk dogs. Credentials. Includes picking up dog poop. Payment in cash required. Call...

Fifteen words *exactly*.

Exhausted, I turn off the light. Who knew writing fewer words would be harder than writing a lot? But now it's done. And since Yee and Anise are meeting me tomorrow morning at CountryWood, everything else will be a snap.

Chapter 8

Monday, 8 AM. My stomach is crawling with roaches. Hard-backed bugs with stiff antennas. Yee and Anise called at seven to say they couldn't meet me today because of cheer practice. I have to interview with the chief of security and the woman who does the newsletter by myself. An outsider, crashing the gates at CountryWood.

I can't do it. I might mess up. They might not like me....

Then I think of my grandpa and feel ashamed. He never let anything stop him. Broken water line. Rusted-out muffler. New pump for the well. *Let's roll up our sleeves and get this done, Sam,* he'd say. *Time's wasting.* If he were alive, he would be proud because I'm interviewing for my first job. My first *real* job. And I'm doing it on my own.

The roaches in my stomach morph to balloons. I'm floating. And to top it off, I get to see the mysterious land of CountryWood.

Because fashion expert Bailey says first impressions are important, I shower, rub deodorant in my armpits, and dress in good clothes. Camo cargo shorts. Blue short-sleeve tee. Crew socks with a matching blue stripe around the top. I *really* want to make a good impression.

What Beth said about CountryWood is what I've heard, too. Rich people live there. Big fancy houses. Private lake for boating. Boats with 100-hp motors. They water-ski and fish, play bocce ball and tennis. Swim in the private pool. Have laptop computers and flat-screen TVs in every room. People with money to burn.

Not like us. Our TV is the old kind with a cathode-ray display that snows perpetually in one corner. We joke about being the only people on the planet to see blizzards in places like Death Valley and the Sahara Desert. Our computer's the old kind, too. A big tower with monster speakers, a fat display.

I strap on my bike helmet. Stretch a bungee cord around my scrapbook. Push off. At the end of the driveway, I meet up with Bailey. She's on her bike, too, ponytail sticking out the back of a pink Razor sports helmet. Her bike is pointed in the opposite direction. We live about three miles from the school in one direction, three miles from CountryWood in the other.

"Where you going?" Spotting the scrapbook, she gets all bouncy. "*Oh,* to see Sid and George. Let's ride together." The smile slides off her face. She's noticed I'm pointed in the opposite direction.

"Uh, I'm not going any place special." Is that a lie? "Where are you going?" A dumb question. She's wearing her cheerleading outfit. Green shirt, purple shorts. Pom-poms in the bike basket.

She doesn't answer. Her eyes are glued on the scrapbook strapped to the rear rack of my bike.

"Hey, gotta go." Rounding the corner toward CountryWood, I look over my shoulder. Bailey's still sitting in the middle of the road, watching me. I wave. She doesn't wave back. I feel like a traitor, but I don't have time to go back and unlie.

I pedal fast, flying past corn and soybean, oat and alfalfa fields. The countryside is a giant chessboard with barns and silos as chessmen. Oak and ash trees mingle overhead, a green umbrella. Sunshine squirms through the leaves, stippling the road. Yellow freckles on blue asphalt. Pollen floats around me, minuscule gliders riding airwaves. Blue jays and cardinals dart through tree limbs; blackbirds and doves line up on power lines.

I put on the brake to slow down. Dark evergreens, stiff and bristly, signal that I've arrived at CountryWood. Planted before the houses were built, they're monsters now. Sentries guarding the entrance. A long white PVC fence stretching along either side guards the rest. The castle wall.

I look at my watch. Right on time. I pull into line behind trucks and vans at the gate waiting to enter. Carpet cleaners. Plumbers. Utility repairmen. Security people inside a small building interrogate drivers, talking through sliding glass panels. Long yellow gate arms raise and lower like magic, permitting entry to those who pass muster.

The outsiders.

To one side of the security hut is another gate. I figure out it's a special one for cars with green stickers on the windshields. Drivers wave a plastic card over an electronic eye and the gate arm raises for them. No security guard. No interrogation. No having to pass muster.

The insiders.

Finally, I reach the front of the line. "Yeah, hey. I'm Sammy Smith and I have an appointment with Mr. Beaumont."

"It's *Chief* Beaumont." A white-haired woman wearing thick glasses scrutinizes my bike. Then me. "You from town?"

"No—yes—I mean, I live in between. Halfway between town and here."

"Anyone lives outside this gate is a Townie." She hands me a piece of orange paper, the size of an index card. A strip of Scotch tape is stuck to the top. "Put this temporary pass somewhere so it's visible. Usually that's on the windshield."

I stick the temporary pass on the handlebar post. "How's that?"

"Make sure you don't lose it," she says, eyes skeptical. "You have to turn it in when you leave." She points a finger at a door and a sign that says SECURITY. "Can't park your bike on the sidewalk or the grass. Leave it in the parking lot."

Geez, even bikes have to follow rules.

I knock on the door that says SECURITY. A reedy voice bellows, "It's open."

Chief Beaumont could be a blocker for the Green Bay

Packers. He's big. *Really* big. A supersized pretzel folded up in an office chair. His skin's the color of milk chocolate. His uniform is khaki brown. A dark-green design is stitched on one pocket, the silhouette of a tree. A badge pinned to his other pocket says CHIEF. He wears a ball cap with the same stitched design above the bill.

I get it. The design represents woods in the country. CountryWood.

I introduce myself. He points me to a chair in front of his desk. I sit. Clutch my scrapbook. Watch as he pulls a piece of paper from a desk drawer.

"Fill out this employment form." He looks at my hands. "That the book Anise and Yee told me about?"

"Yes, sir." We exchange scrapbook and application form. I write in my name, address, and phone number, stop at the line for Social Security number. I pull my wallet out of my pocket, remove my card, and notice he's looking at me. "Um, I haven't learned my Social Security number yet. This is my first time to use it."

The bassoon voice rumbles, "Still have a hard time remembering mine." He continues to turn pages, looking at dogs.

In the place for references, I put down Yee's and Anise's names. For purpose of business, I write, *To walk dogs.*

"Don't have dogs ourselves." Chief Beaumont closes my scrapbook. We exchange it and the employment form again. "Wife keeps two cats, though. Siamese. Independent little buggers, but smart."

I nod. Some of Rosie's cats are part Siamese. Monday and Thursday, the ones Max stopped from eating Birdie.

"Okay." He straightens glasses that look like aviator goggles. The wraparound kind with an elastic strap that goes around your head. "Here are the rules."

I learn that dogs are to be kept on a leash at all times. Are not supposed to bark continuously, as this is considered a disturbance. Are not allowed on the beach or inside the pool area, as their hair clogs up drains. Most importantly, they are not to leave "their business" anywhere.

"Carry plastic bags with you to pick up after them. You know how to do that?"

I nod. He demonstrates anyway. Putting his hand into a plastic bag, he picks up a tennis ball, inverts the bag so the ball's inside, knots the bag so the ball is tied at the end.

"You see how it's done?"

I grin. "Not a problem. I've heard most of the dogs out here are little." I point at the plastic bag in his hand. "Peanuts, not tennis balls."

He lets out a rumbling laugh. *Har-har-har.* The corners of his eyes wrinkle up like bird tracks. I decide he's okay and relax.

"There's bag holders every couple blocks," he says. "Look like birdhouses on short posts but they're filled with recycled plastic bags. Have to carry the bag back to the dog owner's house, throw it away there. And you can't walk the dogs anywhere but on the right-of-way." He pauses, eyeing me. "You know what a right-of-way is?"

"Yes, sir. The strip of grass on the side of the road."

He nods, looking over my completed form. "You don't follow the rules, the dog owners will be given the citation." Another piercing look through the glasses. "You know what *that* means?"

"Yes, sir, I'll be fired." I'm not feeling so relaxed anymore.

He pulls a map out of a different drawer. Points out a lake in the middle. Streets curving around it. Squares that represent tennis courts, swimming pool, beach areas.

"Stay on this loop when you walk the dogs, nowhere else. Leave your bike at the first house you pick up a dog...." He draws a rough circle along certain streets and connects the circle with the line leading back to the front gate. "Pick it up when you're done. Turn in your pass when you leave." He looks at me. "Got that?"

"Yes, sir. Justin Wysocki told me outsiders aren't welcome." I'm glad the outlined route isn't near the places where Justin and his friends will be hanging out. The fun places.

"He did, huh?" Chief Beaumont lets out a deep grunt. "Okay, you're good to go. Any problems, let me know." He points a finger at the door.

"Um, I need to go to the office to place an ad."

"Across the street and down a block."

Outside, I study the map to orient myself. Suddenly, my heart's pounding like a snare drum. On the way to the office, I'll get my first look at the mysterious land of CountryWood.

Mysterious describes CountryWood to a T. It's nothing like I thought it would be. The biggest mystery is why it's called CountryWood.

There's no country or woods anymore. The old oak trees have vanished into thin air. It's like an alien Transformer with front-end loaders for arms descended to Earth and ripped them from the ground. Huge belching machines are digging foundations for new homes and trenches for utility lines. Diesel smoke and fumes float like storm clouds. Light poles are nonexistent, replaced with solar lights along driveways and motion-sensor detectors next to garage doors. Lawn sprinklers work continuously, spraying water on the grass. The only green thing to be seen.

Mom was right. Our place is prettier than this.

Some houses *are* big—two stories with three-car garages—but most are average size, average looking. But all of them, fancy and plain, big and small, are the same distance from the road. *Exactly* the same distance. Lego blocks on steroids, lined up in perfect rows.

I feel like I've entered a parallel universe.

I look at my watch. Nine-thirty and I'm sweating. The sun beats down, a fiery orange globe in a cloudless blue sky. Turning asphalt streets to frying pans. Toasting leaves on the newly planted trees in the front yards. Electric golf carts glide along like enormous slugs, the drivers' faces replaced with metallic sunshades or hidden under hats. I recognize kids from school, carrying beach towels or tennis rackets.

By the time I reach the office, my clothes are waterlogged. My armpits are overflowing sewers. My lips are lizard scales. My memory, though, has sharpened.

Aww, man. I forgot to bring water.

I push through the office door and enter an air-conditioned

room. I pause a minute in the entry, cooling off, and spot an older woman sitting behind a counter, smiling at me.

"Samuel Smith?" she says.

"Yes, ma'am."

"Anise and Yee told me to expect you. I'm Mrs. Callahan. I do the newsletter. Did you bring your ad?"

"Oh, yes, ma'am. It's fifteen words long. *Exactly.*" I pull a wrinkled piece of paper and a ten-dollar bill from my pocket and watch as she reads my ad.

"Well, now, this is very good...." She hesitates. "But I might suggest one change."

Change? The ad is perfect. I worked on it for hours.

"How about we substitute *waste* for *poop* so that the ad reads 'Will walk dogs. Credentials. Includes picking up dog *waste.* Payment in cash required.'"

"Waste? Sure, no problem. I've just heard that's one of the requirements here. You know, picking up a dog's *waste.* So I thought it was important to include it."

"Oh, yes. *Very* important." She slips my ten-dollar bill into a cash box. "I'll make sure this gets in the newsletter. Everyone will have it by this afternoon. We put one in every door."

"That's swell. Um, I hear you might be interested in someone walking your dogs?"

"Yes, indeed. I can't leave the office on Monday, Wednesday, and Friday so my little dogs don't get walked midday. Just morning and evening."

"I, uh, I brought my credentials in case you want to see them." I hold up my scrapbook so she can see it.

She hesitates. "Well, I'm working right now, so it's not a good time. How about you come out tomorrow to meet my little ones? It's important that they also approve of you. And who knows, maybe by then, others will have called and you can meet with them, too. Say, ten o'clock at my house?" She writes her address on a yellow sticky note and hands it to me.

"Yeah, that sounds great." I watch as she starts typing my words into a computer. My ad is now official.

I walk back outside into the glaring sun and head for the security gate. From down the street, someone calls my name. Yee and Anise, still in their cheer outfits, wave me to a stop. Three little dogs sit on a porch behind them, leashes tied to the porch post. Tongues dripping.

"Come over to my house!" Anise yells. "We need a third person so we can practice making a pyramid."

Anise's house is a blue vinyl-clad split-level. Purple petunias spill out of the front flowerbed, the special kind Mom grows that bloom all summer. Her trademark. On one side of the front door is a strange-looking mask that I decide is an *Igbo Mmwo*. Next door is a tan vinyl-clad trilevel, a pagoda fountain in the front yard, and two cement Chinese dragons beside the front door. Yee's house.

I consider their offer, remember Chief Beaumont's orders. "Can't. Have to go straight to the gate when I'm done."

Yee and Anise exchange glances, untie their dogs, and dodge traffic. Sweat stains Yee's shirt and glues her straight black bangs to her forehead. Anise's shirt is sweat-stained, too. Her coffee-brown hair has turned to frizz.

"Walk your bike to the gate and we'll walk with you. I need to exercise Rooster and Rabbit, anyway." Yee pulls two plastic bags from a box on a post and stuffs them in her pocket. Anise follows suit with one bag.

Yee's Pekingese wear different-colored dog halters. The one wearing red darts everywhere. I make a bet with myself that its name is Rooster. The one wearing blue walks quietly beside her. Rabbit. She's matched the colors to the dogs' personalities.

"How did it go?" Anise's toy poodle, Midnight, wears a collar studded with tiny brass bells. "Did you talk to the chief? Mrs. Callahan? Did you get the job walking her dogs?"

I become a limp rag, shoulders and mouth drooping. Watch them go sad-eyed. Say, "Gotcha!" They punch me on the arm and beg for details.

"It went great." I use the back of my thumb to wipe salt crystals from the corners of my mouth. "Chief Beaumont is cool. And

Mrs. Callahan said the paper will go out today—with my ad in it. I'll be meeting her dogs tomorrow at ten o'clock. She couldn't look at my scrapbook today 'cause she's working. And maybe by then, other people will call, too." My shirtsleeve becomes a rag to wipe sweat off my face.

"Didn't you bring water?" Yee stares at the empty bottle holder on my bike. "In this heat, you need to keep hydrated."

Duh.

"Wouldn't hurt to carry some for the dogs, too. I carry a jar lid for Midnight to drink out of." Anise's black poodle jingles happily.

Now, *that's* a good idea.

Yee and Anise grow quiet, staring at me like an expectation hasn't been met. I get it. I'm supposed to say something. But what? Girls are hard to figure out.

"Um…" I clear my throat. "How was the first day at cheer-leading camp?" I wait, hoping I guessed right.

"Awesome—"

"Incredible—"

"Humongous—"

"Inspiring!"

I sigh with relief. Expectation met.

They tell me about their coach and the cheers they learned.

I listen. Nod. Remember Bailey practicing in her front yard. Alone.

"So how come you don't call Bailey to come out and practice making pyramids with you? I mean, she'd be perfect. She lives close, and she's on the cheerleading team, too."

They exchange looks, then stare at their shoes. Adidas, grass stains on the toes. Then Yee gives me a sideways look.

"I think we made her mad. She wouldn't even speak to us today."

"*Mad*—" I'm burning. How can they be so blind? "She's *hurt* 'cause you didn't invite her to practice with you."

Not just them. I remember Bailey again, refusing to wave at me.

They roll their eyes at each other, which burns me more.

I pull to a stop and drop the kickstand. "What do you have against Bailey? Is it because she's fat? She's trying to lose weight, she told the whole class that on Friday. I mean, give her a break. She never says a bad word about anybody—and works her butt off trying to please people."

"But that's just it. She's always *Miss Perky*. It's just..." Anise pauses, eyes flipping through an internal encyclopedia. "Not *normal*."

"That's right. She's in a state of denial." Yee's voice sounds cold. Unfeeling. "No one is happy *all* the time. Why can't she just...I don't know, be herself?"

Yee's been dosing on her dad's psychology magazines again. And now she's Junior Shrink analyzing head problems. Diagnosis? Bailey's screwed up.

I go beyond burning to out-of-control forest fire. "Well, she's not that way with me! I've seen her plenty of times when she wasn't *Miss Perky*."

Like this morning when I lied to her.

"And what about you?" I look at Yee. "Always *Miss Smarter Than Anyone Else*. Tops at everything, even top of the pyramid." I turn to Anise. "And all you ever talk about are amusement parks—*humongous* amusement parks. Did you ever think that the only ones Bailey and I have ever been to are at the county fair? Lots of the other kids, too."

They stare at the ground, chins on their chests. I've lost two more friends.

"Well, if you were Chinese American, you'd understand." Yee looks at me, eyes liquid. "That's the expectation that's put on us. Especially from our family. I just don't want to disappoint them." Damp bangs get pushed aside. "I don't even know who I am either...not really."

Aww, man. I blew it.

"At least you're considered smart." Anise faces Yee. "People are afraid of African Americans 'cause they think we're all gangbangers." She lowers her head, mouth drooping. "And I guess some of us are."

She turns to me. "I'm really tired of going to those amusement parks every summer. When I was little, it was fun. Now I just want to stay home and hang out with my friends. But I don't want to hurt my folks like Saffron did. She, uh...she joined a gang and got pregnant, moved in with her boyfriend. He's a real trick. Won't let my folks see the baby."

"I didn't know." I go from furious to mortified. "How you both felt and all."

"It's okay," Yee says.

"Yeah," Anise says. "You're not a mind reader, how could you know?"

I think about this. "Bailey's not a mind reader, either."

Yee pauses, like she's lost for words. Which is very unusual for her.

"Oh, you mean someone needs to clue her in," Anise says.

"Something like that." Neither one of them says anything. As we start walking again toward the gate, I glance at Yee and Anise, remembering something else. "Hey, thanks for helping me get this job. It's really important."

"Yeah, to buy a dog." Yee shakes her head, frowning. "A *German shepherd*."

"Why do you want *that* kind of dog?" Anise's eyes get big. "I mean, they're so *mean*."

Mean? I wonder if they're talking about Bruno.

"Yeah, well, they don't *have* to be mean." I leave it at that. They'll figure it out.

As we near the security hut, I take a last look at the baking streets, the sticks for trees in the front yards, and say, "Lot cooler at my house. Shady 'cause we have lots of trees."

Watching Yee and Anise wilt, I see an opportunity.

"Yeah, and it's even cooler over at Bailey's. She's got this big oak tree in her front yard where she practices. And her dad keeps their grass like a carpet. A big, soft, *cool* carpet—"

A deafening roar forces us into the ditch. Justin races past in a gasoline-powered golf cart loud as a jet plane. Suddenly, he wheels into a tight U-turn and burns rubber, stopping next to us.

"You're not allowed here." Justin, wearing a black muscle shirt and striped swim trunks, is yelling in my face.

"All legal." I point out the orange pass on my bike. "Arranged everything with Chief Beaumont."

Spotting my dog book on the bike rack, he turns his fury on Yee and Anise. "You helped him, didn't you? You *traitors* helped him get a job so he can trespass on my turf."

His turf? So now CountryWood is the Mysterious Land of Justin?

If I was burning hot before, I'm torched now. "Back off, Justin." My hands ball into fists. Just once, I'd like to put him in his place. Then it comes to me. I *can*.

"And get used to seeing me on *your* turf 'cause I'm getting a job here. And I'm buying a purebred German shepherd puppy this summer, one with a pedigree longer than Bruno's." I stretch out my arm as long as I can make it.

"You're going to regret this, *Spammy*." Justin's face is a scarlet lump.

I respond with an *L* on my forehead.

As he roars down the street, I turn to Anise and Yee. "What's with that guy?"

Anise does a quick shrug. "Just a bully being a bully. He's used to getting his way. His mom and dad buy him and his sister anything they want."

"He wasn't always like this." Yee's brow wrinkles. "We went to the same school in the burbs, and he was a real wuss there. All he did was play video games. But since we moved here...I mean, it's like Dr. Jekyll and Mr. Hyde."

Anise looks at Yee. "It's 'cause he doesn't have to worry about street gangs anymore. I know *I'm* not so scared now."

"But it's not right that he gets away with breaking the rules." I stare down the street where Justin disappeared. "Why doesn't Chief Beaumont stop him?"

"Because Justin keeps track of where he is." Yee taps her head. "We've decided he must have built-in radar instead of a brain."

"So? Why don't you just tell the chief?"

"Won't work if you're a kid. Anyone can say anything about someone else. You know, just to get them in trouble. I guess some of the kids here have done that, so the chief prefers catching someone in the act. After three citations, you get your privileges taken away."

"See, you have to register a golf cart at the office," Yee says, "and fill out a card saying who's authorized to drive it. You break the rules, you can't drive the golf cart anymore."

"But first you have to get caught," Anise says.

"Justin's *never* been caught?"

"*Well...*" She grins. "My dad's good friends with Chief Beaumont, and he heard that Justin has two citations for speeding already. So one more, and..." She uses her hand to pretend she's cutting her throat and chokes out, "*Kaput.*"

"Two! How much does a citation cost?"

"Fifty dollars each. His dad pays for them. They have money to burn."

I see the security gate ahead and say, "Gotta go. The chief gave me strict orders to leave soon as I'm done, and *I* can't break the rules. Besides..." I give them an ear-to-ear grin. "You *two* have to figure out how to make a *three*-person pyramid."

Yee and Anise's eyes bore holes in my back.

Chapter 9

Beth is kneeling next to her Subaru when I get home from Country-Wood, air-pressure gauge in her hand. Lately, she has to put air in the rear tires every couple of days. I glance at the tires as I get off my bike. The tread's gone beyond worn. It's morphed to slick.

"How did it go, little bro?" She looks up at me, dirt smeared on one cheek. "Meet lots of rich people?"

"Went good. Got my ad in the newsletter and have my first customer meeting tomorrow. And I'm sure I'll get other calls."

"Again tomorrow..." She pauses, frowning. "Be home about the same time?"

I look at my watch. "Yeah, 'bout noon, I figure."

"Good. In time to feed Rosie lunch, then."

"No sweat."

"*And* check on Max and Birdie."

Not a question. A command. "*And* Max and Birdie."

Blackmail sucks.

Beth leaves for work, and I do my duty. Max is on alert, watching to see who's coming around the barn. As soon as I appear, he sticks his nose in his water bowl. It's bone dry. The birdbath, too. He nudges me on the leg.

"Okay, okay, I get it."

I rummage around the back porch, find an extra water bowl, and haul a bucket filled with cold water back to the barn. I fill up two bowls for Max and refill the birdbath for Birdie. Max drains one bowl, walks to his empty food dish, and looks at me. Expectant.

"Not time for supper." Max gets Dog Chow morning and night. As I turn for the house, he wags his tail and whines.

Does he want me to stay out here with him?

"No way, buddy. You're the one who fell in love with a bird. You could be lying on the back porch. It's your own fault."

A low whimper trails me like a shadow.

Rosie slams through the screen door, washes her hands in the kitchen sink, and looks at me. Expectant.

I point to her chair at the table.

Lunch is peanut butter and jelly sandwiches, chips, and milk. On real plates and in real glasses. Mom refuses to put more plastic and Styrofoam in the landfill. She won't even use paper napkins. It's her way of saving the planet.

"Did, uh, did Bailey say anything about me?" I can't get Bailey's freckle-spattered face out of my head.

"Bailey doesn't like you no more."

"She said that?"

"Sort of."

Sort of? What does that mean? Remembering the painted-cat disaster, I decide it's time to ask more questions.

"*Exactly* what did she say, Rosie?"

"She said you lied to her, and friends don't do that kind of thing." Jumping down from her chair, Rosie carries her dishes to the sink. She finished her milk, gobbled her chips, but left half the sandwich on her plate. "I'm going back over to Bailey's. We're designing an extra costume."

"Why do you need an extra costume?"

" 'Cause I called the hotel, and Sid said I need two. One for the beauty contest and one for the talent contest. . . ." She pauses, grinning. "But *I* need three."

"How come?" An extra costume means more money for Mom. Money she doesn't have to spend.

"For when I accept the tiara." The kitchen floor becomes a trampoline. "That one's going to be long and glittery and . . . and *splendid*."

Splendid? Where did she come up with that?

"Hold up, Rosie." I envision Justin's little sister practicing Polish dances. Her mother buying designer costumes. *Real* designer costumes. "You know, you might not win."

"That's what Bailey said, too." Rosie leans close and talks in a whisper. "But I *know* I'm going to win." She runs for the door. Giggling.

"Wait! How do you know that...*exactly*?"

" 'Cause you and Sid are best friends." The screen door slams behind her.

Great. My little sister thinks Sid and I have rigged the contest.

"Oh," she says, peering through the screen. "And you're supposed to call him. It's urgent."

I carry my dishes to the sink and eye Rosie's half-eaten sandwich. Mom's always after us not to waste food, but I've already downed two sandwiches and half a bag of corn chips. I could wrap it up, but pb&j sandwiches get soggy fast. Ordinarily, I toss any scraps in Max's food bowl, but that bowl is now behind the barn. A long walk under a scorching sky.

I scrape the sandwich into the trash can and start cleaning up. But the sandwich develops eyes.

Load the dishwasher...

Sandwich stares.

Put the jelly and peanut butter away...

Sandwich stares.

Wipe the table...

Sandwich stares.

"Aww, man." I fish the sandwich out of the trash and carry it to the barn. Max gives me a doggy grin.

"I'm saving the planet," I tell him.

"You said you would call me." Sid's tone is accusing.

Geez, school's only been out three days.

"Yeah, I was going to. I've been kinda busy." I tell him about my job walking dogs.

"Does that mean you're not going to invite George and me over?"

"No. I'll only be working three days a week." The line goes quiet. I decode the silence. "Are you needing out of your cage, Sid?"

"In a very big way, Sam. It is chaotic here. Pageant entries to sort. Entry deposits to keep track of. Phone calls to answer. Questions, questions, and *more* questions about costumes. And my mother changes her mind every day about how to decorate the pageant room. Real plants or plastic. Greenery or flowers. Red carpet or purple for the stage."

"Deposits?" The one word I latch on to. Mom said it cost a hundred fifty dollars to enter the contest. But if she only had to put down a deposit, how much was it? Exactly? "How does that work, Sid?"

"Entrants must put down half the entry fee, which means they pay us seventy-five dollars. The balance is due ten days before the pageant, which is the middle of next month. But it is a nonrefundable deposit, so if someone drops out, we keep it."

"Did my mom put down a deposit yet?"

"Oh, yes. The very first day."

Bummer. That means Mom would lose seventy-five dollars if for some reason she couldn't pay the rest.

"The deposits must be taken to the bank daily because my father worries the money will be stolen. I tell you, the hotel right now is *nuts.*"

I grin into the phone. "Come over tomorrow afternoon. I have to watch Rosie, but she's spending a lot of time over at Bailey's house."

"What time?"

I've never heard excitement in Sid's voice, he's the calmest person I've ever met, but I hear it now.

"Oh, I don't know...round one o'clock. How's that sound?"

"Splendid."

Ha! So that's where Rosie learned that word.

The phone calls Sid mentioned begin to make sense. Especially the ones about costumes. Rosie has to be the costume caller, and now she's decided she needs three. How am I going to convince her she only needs two like everyone else?

All at once, the bell in the plant shed rings. Someone is waiting to be helped.

"Gotta go, Sid. See you tomorrow."

Jogging to the shed, I spot Mom in the driveway. Plaid shirt tied at the waist. Denim shorts exposing rust-colored knees. Ponytail stuck through a ball cap.

If she's home, why does she need me?

Then I see it. A big black SUV that dwarfs our minivan. On the SUV's front window is a green sticker. A Burbie has ventured outside the walled kingdom of CountryWood.

"S'up, Mom?"

Mom's face is bright scarlet. I can't tell if she's steamed, excited, or just hot. The sun is beating down, relentless. A red afternoon.

"Sammy..." Mom pauses, breathing hard. Sweat circles stain her underarms. Dirt ribbons circle her neck. "Grab the end of this flat, help me load it." She points with her eyes at a long plastic tray filled with pots of geraniums. Red. Pink. Fuchsia. Three more flats sit next to it.

I get it. The red face signals excitement. Mom scored a big sale.

We haul the flat to the rear of the SUV, where a suntanned woman stands at the hatch. Helmet of straight brown hair. Snow-white shorts showing off dark tanned legs. A white polo shirt highlighting tanned arms. Arms so muscular she could be on the Olympic rowing team.

"How come she's not helping?" I whisper as we return for the next flat. "Her biceps are bigger than mine."

"Because she just had her *nails* done." Mom's eyes are glinting daggers. "She's throwing a patio party."

Ow! Wrong guess. The red face signals anger. I wonder if

Mom ever had her nails done and decide she wouldn't need to. She keeps them worn down to the quick.

When the next load goes in the van, I chance a look at Mrs. Biceps's fingernails. Miniature rainbows, rhinestone studs on the tips. Money to burn...

By the time we're through loading flats, Mom and I are soaked with sweat, but the back of the SUV is a greenhouse on wheels. A stunning testimony to Mom's hard work.

"As hot as it is..." Mom smiles at Mrs. Biceps. "You'll need to check the soil moisture often. Don't want the plants to dry out and die."

Mrs. Biceps shrugs. "Party's this weekend. After that, it won't matter."

The SUV drives away. Mom's shoulders slump. A fireball goes off behind my eyelids.

"I vote we make those people load their own stuff, Mom— and I'll paint the sign."

"Believe you me, Sammy, there's plenty of times I'd like to do just that." She removes her leather work gloves, permanently shaped like her hands, and tosses them on the potting table. "But if it wasn't for 'those people,' my business would've gone belly up years ago."

I trudge back to the house, hating to admit she's right. But if it weren't for "those people," I wouldn't be getting my puppy, either.

The phone rings right after supper. The call is from a man named Muller who wants to talk to me about walking his dog because he's just had his knee operated on.

"It was outpatient surgery," he says, "but I'll need someone to walk my dog for a while. Depending on how I recover, a few weeks. Maybe longer."

"That'd be great. I'm meeting with Mrs. Callahan at ten. I could meet with you before or after that."

"After," he says, and he gives me his address.

I barely get the phone hung up before it rings again. A man with a name I can't pronounce.

"Pet-drop-a-loss," he repeats, talking slowly. "It is spelled *P-E-T-R-O-P-O-U-L-O-S.*"

I write it down and tell him about my other appointments.

"I am home all the time so come whenever you want."

"Super. Nine o'clock. I'll be there at nine o'clock." I write down his address, too.

I sit by the phone until bedtime, but there are no more calls. But I don't care. My ten-dollar ad has already brought me three customers.

I float all the way upstairs to bed.

Chapter 10

Leaving my bike in the driveway, I ring the doorbell at Mr. Petropoulos's house. Right away, I hear barking—continuous barking—which Chief Beaumont considers a disturbance.

"*Swell*. Just swell." I wonder what I'm going to find on the other side of the door.

"You come in—we sit—we talk—" The words explode from a dark whiskery little man shadowed by a dark whiskery little dog.

I introduce myself, struggle to say his name.

"You call me Mr. P. Lotta people, they have a hard time with my name. Everyone calls me Mr. P."

"That'd be swell." I'm relieved.

Mr. P is short with broad shoulders, muscular arms, and legs so bowed, he rocks side to side when he walks. Unruly gray hair pokes from his head like a porcupine's. Even his flat round ears are hairy. Friendly button eyes shine through a face lined with wrinkles, and white teeth flash when he smiles. Which is a lot. I like him right away.

His whiskery little shadow is another matter. He stopped barking when Mr. P let me in, but now he snarls when I look at him. Lips pulled back, showing pink gums. Teeth that are pointy white spikes. Growl a miniature boat motor sputtering in his throat.

"Fifty years, we have been in this country." Mr. P points to a red velvet chair in his living room and sits down in an identical one across from me.

I perch on the edge of the chair, feeling eyes staring at me. Pictures of people wearing fluorescent halos line the walls. Brass plates and pitchers, dull gold and engraved with designs, fill tabletops. A brightly patterned rug—red and blue, green and yellow—covers the dark wood floor. I feel like I'm in a museum.

"We move here for freedom. In Greece, too much revolution. We escape on a boat by the hair on our chins."

I stare at the spiky stubble on his chin and mumble, "Yes, sir." Wondering who the "we" is that escaped with him, I look down the hallway. Listen for noises in the kitchen. There's silence, except for the little dog with the bristly bark.

Mr. P picks up a plate from a side table and hands it to me. "We have a treat while we talk. I make baklava for us. Baking, it is a hobby." On the plate is a square-looking biscuit with something dripping off it. He picks up an identical plate, takes a bite, and looks at me.

"Uh, exactly what is…bak-la-va?" I flip the biscuit over, watch shiny stuff like Halloween slime string off my fork.

"You never have baklava?" He stares at me like I'm one of the Third World kids on TV. "Greek dessert, honey and nuts. Try it, you will like."

What else can I do? I fork a piece, place it between my teeth, and bite down.

Baklava is delicious. Mr. P talks as I eat.

"We settle in this country after we leave Greece. I help build skyscrapers in Chicago." Chicago sounds like *Ja-car-go* when he says it. "Work on buildings like Sears Tower. Trump Tower. Then I retire. We leave Chicago and move here to the country. The security gate, it makes us safe from gangs. No shootings here. Not so noisy."

Not so noisy? Whiskery dog rumbles like a rocket on a launch pad every time I look at it.

"But we still got delinquents. In April, they wake us up, so I yell at them through the window. What do they do? Break the statue next to our front door. Run away, cackling like laughing jackals!"

Laughing jackals? I get it. He's talking about hyenas.

"Delinquents. Everywhere we live is delinquents."

That "we" again.

"Um, they woke up you and your wife?"

"My wife, she passed on…" He holds up three fingers. "This many years now. We are married fifty years."

"Oh. Sorry." My plate empty, I set it on the table next to me. Mr. P has been so busy talking, he's hardly touched his baklava.

"So." He looks at the scrapbook in my lap. "What do you know about Yorkies?"

Time to show my credentials. I turn quickly through my book and find the page on Yorkshire terriers. My collection is made up of things I've gotten from magazines and the web and glued into different sections. Choosing one of the clippings, I start talking, hoping to pass the test.

"See, this printout tells how the Yorkshire was developed in Yorkshire, England, as a ratter. And this one tells how it was brought to the U.S. in 1878 and became one of the most popular breeds of toy dogs because of its 'sweet expression' and 'cheerful character.' "

I stare at the words *sweet expression* and *cheerful character,* glance toward the dog at Mr. P's feet. It answers with a growl.

"A ratter, huh?" Mr. P raises scraggy eyebrows, looking pleased. "Like me, a hard worker—and an emigrant. After I get off boat, I work very hard, too."

As Mr. P finishes his baklava, I read the same section again to make sure I read it right. I'm surprised that a Yorkie is considered a working dog. All dogs started out as wild animals, but people tamed them and started breeding them to handle different jobs. Hunting. Herding. Protection. Even ratting. Now they're bred for other reasons. As people toys. *Noisy* people toys.

I make eye contact with the Yorkie. He bristles and starts up the boat motor. Ready to tear the big rat in the red velvet chair to shreds.

"I get him a treat so maybe he is happy." Mr. P hobbles to the kitchen.

While he's gone, I do more cramming. I learn that Yorkshire terriers will bark when anything changes—but especially when a stranger enters their living area. I groan as I read another clipping that tells how Yorkies have been known to bark incessantly while being walked on a leash.

Great, just great. In my mind's eye, I see Chief Beaumont writing out a citation.

I chance a look at the dog again, get rumbling in response, and drop my eyes to my scrapbook. Spotting a crumb of baklava on red velvet, I flick it off.

Like I just hit an Off button, the growling stops. Whiskery dog snarfs up the crumb and wags his tail at me.

Aha. I hold my plate close to the floor and let him lick it clean. He jumps in my lap when the crumbs are gone, licking my face.

I laugh. "No, that's all there is. I don't have any more." A happy dog lies down beside me. Man's best friend.

"Hey, he likes you now." Mr. P looks pleased when he sees the dog next to me. "Tell me more." He calls the dog to him and feeds it treats.

"Uh, well, this article tells how the Yorkshire makes a good guard dog despite its size."

Mr. P's eyes shine like bright black marbles. "That is my Apollo, all right. A good guard dog. Anyone comes close to the house, he wake me up...like *that.*" He snaps his fingers.

Apollo. The dog's name is Apollo. I debate whether it's named after the Greek god or the spacecraft that went to the moon. Considering Mr. P emigrated from Greece, I opt for the god. This particular Greek god weighs about four pounds.

Mr. P's eyes turn sad. "See Apollo's belly? Because of no walking, he gets fat. The vet, she says he must walk more." He pats his own stomach, a basketball under his striped T-shirt. "I get fat, too. But my legs, they are not so good for walking anymore. Arthritis in the joints, you see." He pats his knees.

For him, that's bad. For me, it's good.

Mr. P points to my scrapbook again. "You, uh, you going to walk any peekapoos?"

Peekapoos? Why's he asking about peekapoos?

"Um, yes, sir. I'm going to see Mrs. Callahan next. She has two peekapoos."

"Mrs. Callahan is nice lady. We talk about our dogs when I go to the office. *Very* nice lady." His mouth turns downward. "She reminds me of my wife. I miss her very much."

Suddenly, Mr. P slaps his thigh. "Okay. A deal, we got. You start tomorrow, ten o'clock."

"Great." I debate how to bring up the money part. "Um, did Yee and Anise talk to you about salary?"

"Salary? Oh. How much to walk my Apollo." Looking stern, he smacks a fist into the other hand and says, "Five-dollar bill, not a dime more."

"Each time?"

"Each time." Another *smack.* "Not a dime more."

Cool. Fifteen dollars a week for walking a dog that fits in the palm of my hand.

I smack my fist, too, and say, "Not a dime more."

I leave my bike at Mr. P's house like Chief Beaumont told me to do and head for Mrs. Callahan's to meet her two peekapoos. Her house is close by, just down the block and across the street.

Along the driveways, I see lights on posts. Solar-powered LEDs with red, blue, or yellow glass. Some posts are plastic, some aluminum. Others stainless steel. We have a big halogen light on a telephone pole to light our driveway. People at Country-Wood have Christmas lights.

As I walk, I become a calculator, figuring how long it will take to make enough to buy one of the puppies in the newspaper. If I can get fifteen a week for the four dogs, I'll make sixty dollars a week. In a little over four weeks, I'll have two hundred and sixty dollars. Ten dollars more than I need.

Woohoo. I'm a laughing jackal all the way to Mrs. Callahan's.

Chapter 11

When I saw Mrs. Callahan at the office, I couldn't see her very well behind her desk, so I'm surprised when she opens the door. She's as opposite Mr. Petropoulos as summer is to winter. Her hair is sunshine. Cheeks pink rose petals. Mouth a never-ending smile. In a singsong voice, she invites me into a living room filled with flowers that will never wilt. Flowery patterns cover the sofa and chairs. Pictures of flowers hang on walls. Vases of silk flowers fill every table. She introduces me to two white dogs, curly marshmallows with bows on their ears. Baby and Buddy hide behind her legs, growling at me.

"I don't know, Sammy." Mrs. Callahan's smile starts to droop. "I'm afraid this isn't going to work."

But it *has* to work....

"Wait, let me show you what I know about peekapoos." I sit down on the flowery sofa, open my scrapbook, and pause, remembering that Buddy and Baby are designer dogs, not purebred. *And* remembering that Beth gave me a printout about peekapoos.

I flip pages furiously, looking for the printout. It's *gone*.

Mrs. Callahan stares at me. Eyes expectant.

"I'll, uh, I'll have to look at two sections because Buddy and Baby...well, uh, they're not purebreds. They're a mix of poodle and Pekingese."

The golden smile makes another showing. "*Phish*—like I care about purebred?" Mrs. Callahan settles into a flowery chair.

As I did with Mr. P, I talk about the best parts to Mrs. Callahan. She's happy to hear that poodles are considered loyal and playful. That Pekingese, once considered sacred dogs, are dignified and aristocratic.

Buddy and Baby aren't so happy. Neither will come near me. When Mrs. Callahan's smile starts to droop again, my heart pummels my ribs. Silently, I regurgitate what I just read, select the choicest piece, and spit it out before I forget it.

"Buddy and Baby are acting this way 'cause they take more after the Pekingese than the poodle. You know, *dignified*. I'm sure as soon as they get to know me better, they'll warm right up."

"Yes, *dignified*." Smiling again, Mrs. Callahan gives both dogs a treat. Little dog biscuits shaped like bow ties. Then she turns her smile on me and says, "Now, a treat for *us*."

She disappears before I can tell her about the treat at Mr. P's house. As I wait for her, I read a description of the two dogs' temperaments, hoping to find something that will make them like me. I learn that Pekingese are independent, assertive, and stubborn. Poodles, especially the miniatures, are picky and excitable.

A mental picture emerges. Chief Beaumont issuing me another citation for disturbing the peace.

I notice a bunch of dog toys on one end of the sofa and pick up a tennis ball. Immediately, Buddy and Baby are in front of me, ears alert. I toss it across the room, and they make a dash for it. One of them returns it, and I toss it again. They're both gone in a flash.

Mrs. Callahan returns with a tray holding two bowls and a glass of milk. "Oh, you found their weak spot. They both love to chase tennis balls."

One of the dogs brings the ball back to me, covered in slime. I toss the ball again, wipe my hands on my shorts, and take the bowl she hands me.

"What else does it say?" Mrs. Callahan has noticed I've been doing more reading.

I don't answer because I'm looking at what's in the bowl. Vanilla ice cream scooped onto something resembling melted candle wax. Lumpy, mucus-colored candle wax.

She notices my hesitation. "I thought a hot day like today would be perfect for jelly and ice cream. It's a traditional Irish dessert. That's what I am, you know. Irish. I get Granny Smith apples at the orchard—organic, so no sprays—and make the jelly myself." Beaming her smile, she says, "Organic means it's good for you, Sammy."

"Yes, ma'am. My grandma used to make her own jelly, too."

It's my first time for jelly with ice cream topping, but the first bite tells me it's good. *Very* good. I eat fast before the ice cream can melt and use my hand to blot a milky drop off something stuck between my legs. The clipping on peekapoos.

"Look." I hold up the clipping like it's a golden ticket to Willy Wonka's chocolate factory. "This says the peekapoo is a hybrid dog that originated in the United States in the 1950s."

"Oh." Mrs. Callahan claps her hands together. "That's when I grew up. I had a felt skirt with a pink poodle on it and wore saddle oxfords and bobby socks. Now I have to wear these clunky orthopedic shoes."

I look at Mrs. Callahan's feet. Before she mentioned them, all I saw was her smile.

She points to the clipping. "Go on. *Please* go on."

"Yes, ma'am. It says now-a-days some breeders are crossing peekapoos with toy poodles, making an even smaller dog." I glance at Buddy and Baby and estimate their weight at five or six pounds each. A little bigger than Mr. P's Yorkie, Apollo.

"That's exactly what Baby and Buddy are," Mrs. Callahan says. "My *toys*." Her face glows when she looks at the two "dignified" pooches. She hands me the bag of dog biscuits. "Here, Sammy. Now that you've finished *your* treat, you can give Buddy and Baby a cookie. They *love* anyone who gives them cookies."

I give Buddy and Baby three dog biscuits each. I want them to love me a lot. As they sit down in front of me, I notice that one dog's ear ribbon has come loose, so I retie it in a double knot.

"Why, that's very good," Mrs. Callahan says. "Where did you learn to do that?"

"I have a little sister—her name is Rosie. I watch her when

Mom's working and have to tie her hair up all the time." When Mrs. Callahan smiles, I know I've got the job.

"Are you walking other dogs?" Mrs. Callahan asks as I'm bribing her "toys" with more cookies.

"Yes, ma'am. One for Mr. P and a dog for Mr. Muller."

"I talk to them at the office sometimes. They seem like very nice men."

"I've already talked to Mr. P. I start walking Apollo tomorrow."

"Oh?" Suddenly, summer turns to winter. Mrs. Callahan's face becomes a pasty-colored sack filled with flabby mouth, eyes, jaws. Sagging flaps for a neck. "And just how much are you charging to walk Apollo?"

"Five dollars, three times a week. Um, that's five dollars for one dog ... *each* time."

"*Goodness gracious*. That's a lot of money for me. You see, I only get my late husband's Social and the little bit they pay me for working in the office here."

Social. I get it. She's on Social Security—her *husband's* Social Security. My grandma does the same thing. I look around Mrs. Callahan's house. Like Mr. P's, it's nice, but not fancy. Neither of them is rich enough to burn money.

As I try to figure out what to do, I get an idea: I could walk all the dogs at the same time and get through faster.

I tell Mrs. Callahan what I'm thinking. "You see, I can save time by walking all the dogs at once. If you call Mr. P and Mr. Muller and arrange it with them, I'll only charge you five dollars to walk *both* Buddy and Baby. But it has to be three times a week, and five dollars *each* time."

"Oh, that's a piece of cake." Her sagging cheeks lift in a smile. "I'm very good with words. That's why I do the newsletter for CountryWood...." She pauses. "But you'll need to come by the office and pick up my house key so you can get in. And after you're through walking Buddy and Baby, lock them inside and bring it back to me."

"Yes, ma'am, no problem." Grinning, I hand Mrs. Callahan my empty bowl and milk glass. At forty-five dollars a week, I can earn two hundred and fifty dollars in five and a half weeks. Still plenty of time to get a puppy this summer.

Mrs. Callahan, Buddy, and Baby walk me to the door. "I'll call Mr. Muller first," she says. "That way, everything will be all set by the time you meet him."

"Great."

"And, uh..." Mrs. Callahan pauses, her smile wavering. "Don't worry about Mr. Muller's bearing. I sense that underneath, he's a nice man. Just lonely, like the rest of us."

Underneath? What does that mean?

Chapter 12

Mr. Muller looks like he just stepped out of Hogwarts Castle in the Harry Potter movies. Dark eyes. Pale skin. Wire glasses pinching his nose. His house is filled with dark leather chairs, dark tables with stout legs, and dark bookshelves stuffed with books.

Siegfried is a muscular brown dog with black ears sharpened to a point and dark eyes that never blink. He looks to weigh only nine or ten pounds, but for a little dog, he's intense.

How can a dog that doesn't bark be more intimidating than one that does?

Right away, I learn that Mr. Muller is really Dr. Muller. Not the kind of doctor that prescribes pills, but the kind that teaches you. And he prefers that I call him *Professor* Muller.

"I taught medieval studies, specializing in myth and legends." He runs fingers along the crease in his dark trousers. Straightens the stiff collar on his gray shirt. "Do you know what that is, Samuel?"

"Yes, sir. Stories about dead heroes and stuff."

"*Stuff*—" Professor Muller makes a choking sound, his Adam's apple moving up and down like it's on a mechanical pulley. "But you are in part correct. Siegfried was named for a Germanic mythical warrior hero."

"He was?" I glance at the dog, who looks awfully small to be a warrior, then at Professor Muller. "Mr. P named his dog after Apollo, but I can't remember what he was the god of."

"Apollo was the Greek god of music, poetry, and many other things." Because of his knee, Professor Muller has to use a cane to get around. Stiffly, he shuffles to his bookshelves, which line three walls in his living room. A minute later, he returns with a small dark book.

"This will acquaint you with some of the more popular heroes, gods, and goddesses. You may keep it, as I have no further need of it." He sits down again, resting his leg on a footstool. "And now let me see the book you have brought."

I open my scrapbook to the section on miniature pinschers and begin. "Well, for short, miniature pinschers are called Min Pins and they came from Germany. They're real popular as watchdogs and house pets—"

Without warning, Dr. Muller leans toward me and takes the book from my hand. "I am quite capable of reading for myself," he says.

"Yes, sir." I sit quietly, watching him read. Siegfried the warrior dog sits quietly, watching me. Seconds pass. Then minutes. Professor Muller reads everything I've collected about Min Pins. Then he sighs, cheeks hollow. Face unhappy. I wonder if my scrapbook didn't pass the test. If *I* didn't pass the test. How I could have made it better.

I breathe deep. "You, uh, you don't like the scrapbook?"

"No, it is good, actually." He taps the scrapbook with a yellowed fingernail. "A thorough job. I would give you an A- for completeness, a B+ for organization." He pauses, looking through the pages again. "And a B for neatness. You could have used a little less paste." He peels a dried blob of Elmer's glue off the corner of a clipping.

I let out the breath I didn't realize I was holding. "Thanks. My older sister helped me. She works a lot with animals and wants to be a veterinarian."

"A vet, you say."

"Yes, sir. She's leaving for college in the fall."

He nods slowly. "And have you learned how to care properly for animals from her? That could be a big advantage for someone who walks dogs."

"Oh, yes, sir. She's taught me a lot. And I've taken care of an old dog for years. He's probably not going to be around much longer, though. I'm going to buy my own dog when I have enough money. And I'll take care of it, too."

"Is that why you're working?"

"Yes, sir." I pause, noticing he's still not smiling. "I'd take real good care of Siegfried, and watch him extra close."

"Oh, I'm sure you would." He taps a section of one page and sighs again. "*This* part is what saddens me." Straightening his glasses, he points to a clipping. "It tells how the breed needs a daily walk on a lead, or short hours of free exercise in a safe area." He closes the book with a *clap*. "In the university town where I lived, there was such a place. A fenced area to take our dogs where they could run free. Now . . ." He waves his hand like he's casting a spell. "We pay for many, many amenities here—swimming pool, tennis court, boat docks—and yet we don't have a dog run."

As an ornate clock on the mantel chimes the half hour, Siegfried places a paw on the footstool.

"*Ah*. Time for Siegfried's walk. We follow a strict regimen here. Breakfast at eight, lunch at noon, dinner at six. Walks at midmorning and midafternoon. Regrettably, the routine has been interrupted."

I notice the dog leash lying on the footstool and pick it up. Immediately, Siegfried is at my side. Ears raised. Mouth open, panting.

"He may need to go outside," Professor Muller says. "I've been putting him on a rope just outside the back door. It's long enough for him to do what he needs to do and get a little exercise, but not nearly enough. I'll let him out as soon as we finish our business."

"No walk today," I say, rubbing the dog's head. "Maybe tomorrow . . ." I look at Professor Muller.

"Yes, perhaps . . ." Professor Muller pulls a plastic bag containing dog biscuits shaped like little bones from his pocket. "I worry so much about Siegfried." He rubs the dog's head.

"Why?" Siegfried looks to be four or five years old and healthy. "Is he sick?"

"Certainly not! I make sure he is properly cared for." He hands me the bag so I can give the dog a biscuit, too. "I worry that I will die before he does. I don't want him ending up in a cage at a pet store." He looks at me. "You've seen them. Cages with signs on the front that describe the animal's character traits. The kind of home it would do well in."

"Yes, sir." As Siegfried munches down a dog biscuit, I picture him in a cage with a sign that says WARRIOR DOG ACCUSTOMED TO A STRICT REGIMEN. ENJOYS GERMAN MEDIEVAL STUDIES.

Oh, yeah, he'd be adopted in a heartbeat.

For some reason, I think of Max, envisioning the sign that would go on his cage if he were being adopted. BIG SMELLY DOG WITH GARBAGE DISPOSAL FOR STOMACH. PRONE TO EXPLOSIVE ERUPTIONS OF NOXIOUS GASES AND BILIOUS AIR. His chances of adoption would be as bad as Siegfried's.

No, worse. Which is why he ended up with us.

"Well, maybe someone would adopt him. That's how we got our old dog. He's been living with us four years now."

"Is that so?" Professor Muller nods, looking thoughtful. "Well, clearly, he found a good home." He looks at me, eyes unswerving. "All right then, it's settled. Mrs. Callahan called and explained the terms and I find them agreeable...on one condition. That you also pick up the waste in my backyard on those days that you come. I should be able to handle that job myself in a few weeks, but not right now. Is that agreeable to you?"

"Yeah, sure. Great. *Super*-great." I stick out my hand for a handshake to clinch the deal. Professor Muller's fingers are all bones. His knuckles are knotty knobs.

Professor Muller accompanies me to the door, his back a steel girder. "Until tomorrow, Samuel." But as the door closes, the wooden face cracks open in a smile.

I grin. Mrs. Callahan pegged Dr. Muller right.

I sprout wings after I pick up my bike and head for the security gate. Flying around golf carts, cars, trucks.

I've done it.

Suddenly, I hear a golf cart, the gasoline-powered kind. I stop pedaling and push my bike onto the right-of-way. Seconds later, Justin comes speeding up.

"I'm gonna get you, Spammy!" he yells. He spins around as the security gate comes into view, driving off fast.

Chief Beaumont walks outside when I turn in my pass. The ball cap is pulled low to keep off the sun's glare. Curly black hair, starting to gray at the temples, pokes out around his ears. "How'd things go, Sam?"

"*Solid*. I'll be walking dogs Monday, Wednesday, and Friday. Starting tomorrow at ten o'clock."

He nods toward the woman at the window. "Bertha here will have a pass waiting for you." The woman behind the sliding glass panel smiles at me.

I smile, too, then hesitate, wondering if I should mention Justin's threat.

"Something else, Sam?" Chief Beaumont's eyes slice through his glasses.

I shake my head. But on the way home, I think about Justin a lot. I can't remember a time he got into it with anyone at school in the three years he's been here. *Really* got into it. Not one black eye. Or bloody nose. A shoving match. He won't even play contact sports. But at CountryWood, he's the Terminator.

And now there's a new bull's-eye painted on his target.

Me.

Chapter 13

Sid arrived right on time Tuesday afternoon, with George. For the last half hour, George has been investigating the inside of Rosie's blue plastic wading pool. Like a corral, its walls keep him contained. A jar lid serves as a water bowl.

Gerbil heaven.

Sid insisted we drag the pool around to the barn because he wanted to see Max guarding Birdie. But right after we got there, he asked to look at my dog scrapbook. His head has been stuck in it ever since. And as he turns the pages, he looks toward Max.

"How long did it take you to get here?" I pull grass, toss it in the wading pool, watch George nibble.

"Twenty-five minutes, maybe thirty."

"That's not too bad. 'Bout the same time it takes to get to CountryWood."

Sid turns more pages.

"George is glad to get out of his cage." I pull a dandelion, toss it into the wading pool, watch George push it around like a soccer ball.

Sid nods his reply. Turns another page.

I swat at a fly. Scratch an itch. Blow out my breath. "What *are* you looking for, Sid? The section on Chihuahuas is closer to the front. I made the book alphabetical."

"Yes, I read about Chihuahuas...." He turns another page, glancing toward Max. "But I am determining Max's breed."

That makes me laugh. "Max doesn't have a breed, Sid."

He looks at me, poker-faced. "Sam, *all* dogs start out as some breed."

"Well, yeah, I know that, but…"

"I believe Max is Bouvier des Flandres and Schapendoes. And perhaps some Pyrenean sheepdog."

"You're kidding." Sid's face says he's dead serious.

"Look here." He begins to talk, pointing out sections in my dog book as he turns pages. "You see, it tells how the Bouvier des Flandres originated in Belgium, France, and the Netherlands."

Sid pronounces the name so that it sounds like Boo-vee-ay duh Flahnders. Since he's one of the smartest kids in class, I figure he knows.

"It says the Bouvier is square built with a big head and a large nose, high-set ears, and dark brown eyes covered with long eyebrows that give the dog a melancholy look." Another glance at Max. "I think Max looks very melancholy."

I look at Max. See stringy hair. A long tongue drooling slime.

"And further, *Bouvier* means 'cowherd' in French." Sid gives me a satisfied look.

"Look around, Sid." I laugh. "You see any cows?"

"Obviously not, but I think Max has substituted birds for cows." He frowns. "I do find it a bit strange that he has switched his loyalty to birds."

It's because you told Max to pester someone else, the voice in my head whispers.

"And…" Sid turns to the section on Schapendoes and pronounces the syllables carefully. "The *SHA-pone-dues* is similar looking, but smaller, and the coat is blue-gray in color. It is very loyal to its owner." He looks at Max again. "In this case, that would be a bird."

I look at Max, too. His coat *is* bluish gray, except around his mouth where the hair has turned white. *Snow* white.

Max is getting old. *Real* old.

"And here…" Sid turns to another section of my dog book. "The Pyrenean sheepdog"—pronounced *Pi-REN-e-an*—"is also from the same part of the world as the Bouvier. Its color is basically gray, often tipped with grayish silver, white, or yellow. It, too, has a black nose, but its eyes are chestnut." He looks at me. "What color are Max's eyes?"

"I don't know." I hunch my shoulders. "What color's a chestnut?"

Sid raises his eyebrows. "The color of a chestnut nut, Sam."

"Sid, I've never seen a chestnut nut."

Sid rolls his eyes, walks to a chinquapin oak tree, and returns with fuzzy nut he picked up off the ground. Peeling off the husk, he holds up a glossy red-brown nut. "A chestnut nut."

"Oh. We call those hairy acorns."

Together, we walk over to Max and lift the hair so we can see his eyes.

"Chestnut," Sid says, looking smug.

"So . . . *what?* You're saying Max is a . . . a Boo-sha-peer."

Sid grins. "That's very good, Sam. I like it."

"I was kidding, Sid," I groan. "You don't find any of those breeds around here—much less all three."

"Do you know Max's history?"

"Well, no. I think he was found running loose. You know, a stray."

"Then perhaps he did not come from around here. I, too, am different. Why? Because I emigrated here from India."

Even nonsense makes sense when Sid says it. Then I wake up. "That's crazy, Sid. All you've done is mix up a bunch of different breeds."

"So? Until a few years ago, I had never heard of a Shi-poo, a labradoodle, or a Morkie."

"A Morkie?"

"Yes. A cross between a Maltese and a Yorkshire terrier."

"You just made that up."

"One of our motel guests last week had a Morkie. He paid six hundred dollars for it."

I should have known better. Sid never makes things up.

Besides, he's right again. The peekapoos I'll be walking at Country-Wood are a made-up breed.

Correction: *designer* breed.

"What are you doing?" Rosie runs around the corner of the barn, and she's not alone. Bailey is with her, and she's smiling.

Sid quickly explains how we have concluded that Max is a Boo-sha-peer.

"Wow." Rosie gives Max a wide-eyed look. "That's elegant."

Elegant. Another word that sounds like it came out of a British news commentator's mouth. Namely, Sid's.

As Sid shows the appropriate pages in the dog book to Rosie, Bailey sits down next to me. She's wearing one of her creations, a yellow-and-purple tie-dyed tee, and her feet tap the ground like two drumsticks wearing Converses. She's bursting to tell me something.

"Yee and Anise called." Soft whispering. "They might be coming over to practice at my house on Tuesdays and Thursdays. You know, opposite days we have cheerleading. They said you told them I have a good place to practice."

"Well, you do." I shrug like it's not important. Inside, I'm all shouts.

"But you didn't have to tell them."

"It was the truth."

"They're biking over today to see how long it takes them"—she pauses, frowning—"and to see if they think it would work out. I told them Rosie and I would be over here 'cause Sid was coming out."

Just then, I see two bikes pull into the driveway. Yee and Anise walk into the backyard, looking hot and sweaty. I motion them over.

"Gee," Anise says, looking around the backyard. "This is like a park." She sits down next to Sid.

"It is?" I look around our backyard to see if something has changed. It hasn't.

"Really, it is." Yee sits down next to Anise. "So big and green.

Not just the grass, but…*everything*. And your mom's flowers are beautiful." She indicates Mom's perennial garden. "This is a lot prettier than CountryWood."

Just what Mom said….

"I think so, too," Sid says. "Much more pleasant than our asphalt parking lot." He catches everyone up on Max's new pedigree as a Boo-sha-peer.

"Doesn't that make Max sound *splendid*." Bailey gives Anise and Yee her smiley-face grin.

Anise and Yee roll their eyes.

Translation: Bailey's being too "perky."

"He would be much more splendid if he were clean." Sid wrinkles his nose at Max, who is doing his thing. Lying in a heap. Imitating a pile of dead leaves. Emitting foul odors.

Looking at his watch, Sid puts George back in his cage.

"Where you going?" Rosie says, eyes wide. "I didn't get to play with George yet."

"I must be home before three o'clock. That is when we eat dinner."

"Three o'clock?" I stare at Sid. "You eat at three o'clock?"

"Yes. We must have the smell out of the lobby before check-in time. That starts at four o'clock." Sid's face blooms rosy pink. "You see, we enjoy our food with a lot of spices, and some of our guests find the smell repulsive."

I walk Sid to his bike and watch as he straps George's cage on the back. A blue bandanna serves as a sunshade.

"Thank you for inviting me over, Sam. Perhaps George and I can come back again?"

"Sure. How 'bout every Tuesday and Thursday?"

"*Splendid.*"

Suddenly, I have an idea. "Hey, I could use a favor, Sid." I tell him how Rosie thinks she's a shoo-in to win the pageant because he and I are friends.

"Oh, that is a very big problem. Have you explained to her that she may not win?"

"Sure, but I'm her brother. Sisters never listen to brothers."

He nods, looking sympathetic. "If you think it would help, I can talk to Rosie. I will explain that we are only supplying the space for the pageant, nothing more. The judges are unknown to us."

"*Solid.*"

Sid wheels off, George's blue sunshade rippling behind. I wait until he reaches the corner, wondering if he will turn to wave. He does.

I grin. Three big problems solved in one day. Bailey isn't mad at me anymore. Sid's going to straighten out Rosie's thinking about the pageant. And Yee and Anise are going to start practicing with Bailey…maybe.

I return to the backyard, feeling good. But I'm the only one smiling when I get there. I look around and see that Rosie is gone.

"Where's my little sister?" I sit down next to Yee. Anise is next to her, and Bailey sits across from us.

"Making lemonade," Bailey says, grinning big. "She said your mom buys the packaged kind that gets mixed with cold water and ice because it's healthier than soda pop." She looks at Yee and Anise again. "Isn't that cool—I mean, their mom is *so* into this healthy food thing! Wish I could be more like her. I'm into ice cream…and cookies…and mayo. Geez…" She grins bigger. "I just love mayo. I put mayo on everything. Sandwiches and hamburgers—I even dip French fries in mayo. Do you do that? Dip French fries in mayo?"

Yee and Anise look at their shoes.

Bailey grins bigger.

I nudge Yee in the ribs.

Yee glares at me, then turns to face Bailey. "Um, why do you do that?"

"You mean, dip French fries in mayo?" Bailey's grin is plastic now.

Yee nudges Anise in the ribs.

"No." Anise glares at Yee. "*Smile* all the time."

"Yeah," Yee says, her voice sounding stronger. "You know, you don't have to be so...*perky* all the time."

"Perky?" The plastic smile slides off Bailey's face. She's figured out that she's on trial. "Because that's what fat kids do," she says. "I mean, we're not pretty, so we have to be...*perky*."

"*Huh.*" Anise looks at Yee and me. "Did you know that? I didn't know that."

I hunch my shoulders and look at Yee.

"But doesn't your mouth get tired?" Yee stares at Bailey. "My mouth would ache if I grinned like that all the time."

Things are so quiet, you can hear the wind blowing through the trees. All at once, Bailey falls back on the grass, arms flopped out to her side.

"Ohmigosh, *yes!*" she cries. "Sometimes my cheeks hurt so bad, I think they're gonna fall off my face. I *hate* smiling all the time." She sits up quickly, looking between Yee and Anise. "But just 'cause I'm fat doesn't mean I'm not strong. I mean, I could be part of a pyramid easy 'cause my folks make me do chores— *outside* chores. Under all this fat is *muscle*." She flexes her arm, showing off her bicep. "You wanna feel?"

"No," Anise says, pushing Bailey's arm away. "It's just that... well, it's okay not to smile so much, especially when we're practicing."

"And at cheer practice," Yee says. "And in school...and after school...and during gym...and—"

"All the time, Bailey," I say. "They're saying just be yourself all the time. You know, like you are when you're with me?"

"Oh, is that all?" Bailey raises her shoulders, lets them drop. "Sure."

And before I know it, they're all smiling at each other. Real smiles, not plastic.

"What's so funny?" Rosie sets a sloshing pitcher of lemonade on the picnic table.

"You wouldn't understand," I say, and run to the house to get glasses.

After they've finished their drinks, Yee and Anise get up to leave.

"See you at camp tomorrow," Yee says to Bailey.

"Yeah, and on Thursday to practice," Anise says. "At *your* house."

"*Cool*," Bailey says.

I walk Yee and Anise to the road. "That *was* cool, guys." I grin. "Real cool."

I watch until they reach the corner that leads to Country-Wood, and then I head back to the house, where Rosie and Bailey are cleaning up the lemonade stuff.

"What are you doing?" When I get there, I find the lemonade and glasses still on the picnic table and Max standing in the middle of Rosie's wading pool. Lapping soapsuds.

"Giving Max a bath." Bailey holds a bottle of oatmeal soap. "And then we're going to brush him."

"Yeah. And now that he's a real dog, he needs to smell better," Rosie says. "Just like Sid said."

Real dog? Max looks like a wet, overgrown rat and smells as bad. No matter what Bailey and Rosie do to him, he'll never be a *real* dog.

Like a pedigreed German shepherd...

Decision time. I've been checking the want ads regularly. The puppies are still being advertised. Now that I have a job, I need to act. Fast.

"But Max needs some chlorophyll dog biscuits." Bailey wrinkles her nose. "His breath definitely is *not* splendid."

"Yeah, whatever."

Hurrying to the house, I find the phone number in the want ads and dial.

The phone rings. And rings.

My stomach ties up in knots.

What if no one's there? What if the puppies are gone?

Chapter 14

"Kendall's Kennels. This is Alice Kendall. Can I help you?"

"Yeah, hi. This is Sammy Smith. *Sam* Smith. Do you still have the German shepherd puppies for sale?"

Mrs. Kendall tells me they have three males and a female puppy available.

"That's great! I'll take one of the males. I can pay you ninety dollars now and the rest when I get it."

"You want to give me part payment and take a puppy home...." A long pause on the line. "Sorry, we don't do business that way."

What? But I bragged to Justin that I'm getting a puppy—in front of Yee and Anise.

"Well..." My mind races. "How 'bout this? I'll give you a ninety-dollar *nonrefundable deposit* and pay you some each week. I'll take the puppy when we're all paid up."

Mrs. Kendall laughs. "We don't do layaway, either. When you get the money, give me a call back."

My tongue feels like Jell-O that's set in the refrigerator a week. Rubber jerky. This isn't going the way it was supposed to.

"How old are you, Sam? I've never sold a dog...sight unseen."

I tell her I just turned twelve. She suggests I bring my parents out to her kennel. That there are things a dog buyer needs to do to protect himself.

"Like what?"

"Like making sure a dog is what the breeder says it is. Don't get me wrong, our dogs have great pedigrees. We keep a clean kennel, keep our dogs healthy. Make sure they're bred right. But not all breeders do that. Have you heard of puppy mills?"

When I don't answer right away, she goes on talking.

"You understand, of course, that I will have other potential buyers calling me."

My heart pounds. "Are . . . are you saying you'll sell the puppies to them if they have *all* the money?"

"That's what we're in the business to do, Sam. Sorry."

The *click* almost punctures my eardrum. I return to the kitchen, feeling like I've been run through the garbage disposal.

"What's to eat?" Rosie slams through the screen door, oozing puddles.

"Take off your shoes. You smell like a wet rat. And change clothes before Mom comes in."

"You're being bossy, Sammy. I'm gonna tell."

"Go ahead, I don't care."

Rosie turns her back, ignoring me.

"And you need to be taking care of *cats*." I start talking more loudly as Rosie heads for the stairs. "Not some dumb old dog."

"Already fed them. Max is hungry and Birdie needs water. Her birdbath is dry."

Great. Now a six-year-old is telling me what to do.

"Where's Bailey? She had time to haul water for Max's bath. She can water him and Birdie."

"Gone home to work on my costumes. I'm going over for a fitting soon as I change." Rosie stomps upstairs, her footsteps echoing through the house.

The kitchen grows quiet, so quiet I can't stand it. I slam through the screen door to do chores.

Beth's Subaru clatters into the driveway as I'm filling a water bucket. I wave her over.

"S'up, Sammy? I'm beat." Beth smells of disinfectant. A smear of something dark stains her jeans. Medicine. Puke. Maybe manure. Strands of wavy blond hair string down her neck like wet noodles. "Max all right? He still taking care of Birdie?"

"*Max* is fine. Walk with me around back. I need to ask you a couple things."

I pick up the pail of water. Beth picks up Max's food dish and falls into step beside me.

"What's so important it can't wait till supper?"

"First, tell me about puppy mills."

"Puppy mills?" She frowns, looking bewildered. "Why do you need to know about puppy mills?"

I hunch my shoulders. "Someone was talking about them today."

"Oh. Well, here's the CliffsNotes version. They're also called puppy farms and puppy factories. They're dog breeding facilities operated under inhumane conditions. The female dogs are caged all the time, not allowed to exercise or play. Sometimes they even have to go to the bathroom in their cages."

"Even purebred dogs?"

"That's what puppy mills specialize in, although they're not careful about the breeding process. They don't vet their animals properly, either. As a result, the puppies that are born may have health or behavior problems. When a dog is caged up all the time, it doesn't learn to socialize with other dogs. Or people."

I think about this as we walk. "Is that what was wrong with Max? 'Cause he was caged?"

"Possibly." She thinks a bit, too. "Other dogs just don't do well in cages and go bonkers when they get out. Max being a herding breed could account for it, too."

Herding breed. Beth had already figured out what kind of dog Max was. "How can someone be sure they aren't buying a dog from a puppy mill?"

"Well, those kinds of breeders typically sell through newspaper ads or pet stores, even the Internet. That way buyers can't see how the dogs are treated. A buyer needs to buy a dog from a good place."

"How do you know you're buying from a good place?"

"The best way is to visit the breeding facility, check out the conditions and the breeder."

Just what Mrs. Kendall said. How am I going to check out their kennel? I don't even know where it is.

"Um, what do you know about Kendall's Kennels? I think it's somewhere around here."

"Other side of the county. Solid reputation. Went out there once with one of the vets to check a dog."

If Beth says Kendall's is okay, that's good enough for me. I've found a good kennel, now all I need is money.

Beth looks at me, eyes curious. "Everything all right, Sammy?"

"Splendid. Everything's just splendid."

"Splendid?" She grins. "Rosie's been using that word a lot lately, too."

"Yeah, well. We've been hanging with Sid Patel."

"That's cool. Your vocabulary could use some sprucing up."

"Whatever." I take a breath, go for it. "Um, I know you bought your own car..."

"Yeah..."

"And you've been working to save money for college..."

"Yeah" again, but slower.

"Well, I've found a great deal on a puppy, but I'm a little short. So I was wondering if you could loan me a few dollars."

"What's a few dollars?"

"Two hundred fifty."

"Geez, Sammy. That's more than a *few*. Why can't you wait until the end of summer when you've earned enough?"

" 'Cause Kendall's doesn't do layaway."

Beth stands still. "Mom was worried you wouldn't make enough working at CountryWood to buy a puppy. What if you couldn't pay me back?"

"I will—I promise. I've got customers already. I mean, what could go wrong?"

Beth starts walking again, blinking.

She's gonna do it, she's gonna loan me the money....

Beth's head starts to shake. The kind of headshake that spells trouble.

"Sorry, Sammy. I just put a deposit on a dorm room in

Colorado and need to budget for books and supplies. Could go ten or twenty bucks, but not that much. I'm maxed out, little bro." She looks at me again. "Have you asked Mom?"

"She's paying for Rosie's pageant, remember?"

"Oh, yeah—" Beth pulls up short as we round the barn. "Is that Max? Wow, he looks *great*. About time he had a bath—*past* time. He hasn't been groomed since I took him in for his shots and a bath at the vet's months ago."

The dirty pile of sticks and brush has morphed into a silky-coated dog.

"Bailey and Rosie did it. It was Sid's idea."

"Well, keep it up. It's good for his coat." She walks over, rubs Max's head. "He feels good, too. You can tell by the way he's acting."

Max's eyes and ears are alert. His mouth is wide in a doggy grin. And he twists and turns like a puppy.

"Yeah, but his breath would stop a freight train. I think his teeth are rotted 'cause he's old. *Real* old."

Beth squeezes Max's jaws open, examines his teeth. "Teeth still look pretty good, not too worn down. Some plaque buildup, but dog biscuits would help that. I'll bring some home."

"With *chlorophyll?*"

"No, charcoal. That's what we use for treats at the clinic. Works better than chlorophyll." She looks at Max again. "I swear, this dog's a miracle. First he doesn't die like he's supposed to, and now he's acting like a puppy."

Miracle. That's what Sid said the last day of school.

"Good job, Sam." Beth smiles at me.

"Me? I didn't do anything."

"Get serious. You're the one who turned him around, and he knows it. That's why you're his alpha person."

"*Alpha* person?"

"Alpha is the first letter of the Greek alphabet. Alpha *person* means you're number one with him, the person he respects the most."

Huh. All I was trying to do was stop him from eating my socks.

"Meet you inside." Beth walks back toward the house. "I'm so hungry, I could eat a cow. And that's saying a lot, since I'm a vegetarian."

My heart is a boat motor in my chest. A heavy throbbing lump of metal. Nothing is working out for me. Beth was my last hope…

Unless I can convince Mrs. Kendall to hold a puppy for me.

Chapter 15

Wednesday. 10:24 AM. Four dogs on leashes, each with internal compasses aligned to different magnetic fields. Siegfried's points north. Apollo's, south. Buddy's, sort of east. Baby's, sort of west. Hairy yo-yos, I reel them out and pull them back in. Continuously. Finally, we reach a truce.

Well trained, Professor Muller's pinscher, Siegfried, shadows my left heel. Having the shortest legs, Apollo, Mr. P's yorkie, shadows Siegfried. Mrs. Callahan's peekapoos, Baby and Buddy, take turns in the lead. My eyes are bouncing balls, ricocheting from one dog to the next. My ears are finely tuned hearing aids listening for sounds coming from behind. Cars. Trucks. Bikes. Battery-powered golf carts are the real menace. Gliding as silent as Luke Skywalker's landspeeder, they're on top of us without warning.

One of my back pockets is stuffed with plastic bags. The other holds a lid from a mayonnaise jar. A water bottle is clipped to my left belt loop. So far, I've only picked up after Siegfried. That bag is tied to a belt loop on my right hip. A green plastic bag sporting a Piggly Wiggly logo is filled with Min Pin peanuts. Three more to go, but there's plenty of time. We're only halfway around the loop Chief Beaumont mapped out.

The dogs aren't yapping at all, so I stop worrying about citations for creating a disturbance. It's because of the heat. The dogs can't breathe and bark at the same time. Even though it's midmorning, they pant nonstop. Dogs sweat through their footpads, but when it's really hot, the footpads can't keep up. So they pant. Tongues drooling elastic bands.

I'm not panting, just oozing through all my pores. The dry spell and hot temperatures are cooking everything. Flowers in gardens we walk past have dried to yellow stalks. The asphalt smells like hot tar. The sun's glare is blinding. My face and neck are sunburned. I feel lucky to have worked out a morning schedule, not afternoon.

Buddy and Baby decide to do their business at the same time. I tell Siegfried to sit, reel in Apollo, remove two bags from my pocket. And wait. This part of the job can't be rushed. Serious business for dogs. Nose to ground, sniffing along an invisible line that leads to treasure, no stopping until they find the X that marks the spot. Siegfried took five minutes locating his X. While I wait, I unclip my water bottle and take a long drink. Siegfried looks up at me.

Is he asking for a drink?

"Wait until Buddy and Baby are done." I rub his head. "If I give you a drink now, they'll forget what they're supposed to do." He sits down at my feet, staring at Baby and Buddy.

Is he telegraphing them a message? "Dogs aren't *that* smart . . . are they?"

Great. I'm talking to myself—about stupid things. Bored with waiting, I decide to test the theory.

"Siegfried, tell Apollo to do his business now because it would save time."

Siegfried looks at Apollo and pants harder. Apollo lies down on the ground.

I laugh.

After Buddy and Baby find their treasure spots, I pull out the jar lid I brought for a water dish. As the dogs are taking their turns, I hear a noise. A loud roaring sound on the next street over.

Justin is on the prowl.

Siegfried stands alert, looking toward the noise. Apollo

starts to whine. Just then, Baby and Buddy finish drinking. I look around, searching for cover. Some thick bushes or a clump of trees to hide behind. Barren yards and black asphalt stare back at me.

Maybe he doesn't know I'm here. Maybe he won't find us....

Hurriedly, I pick up the two peanut-size piles that Buddy and Baby deposited. Just as I finish tying twin Walmart bags to a belt loop, the roaring noise grows louder. I look up and see a golf cart spinning around the corner, a pilot-guided missile. Stuffing the jar lid in my pocket, I yell to the dogs, "Run!"

But it's no use. A dog's ability to cover ground is determined by how long its legs are. I'm walking four very little dogs with very short legs. Being the biggest, Siegfried is the fastest. He manages to keep up with me. Buddy and Baby tangle their leashes and trip over each other. The smallest of them all, Apollo, is stretched at the end of his leash—behind me. I'm dragging him like a hairy little red wagon.

When the noise behind us reaches the pitch of a jet engine, I pick up Buddy, Baby, and Apollo. "Hurry, Siegfried!" I yell. *"Hurry!"*

We run.

Justin swerves off the road in front of us, forcing us into the ditch. I stumble over Siegfried's leash and land in the middle of a dog pile. A *yelping* dog pile.

Justin yells, "I warned you, *Spammy!*" He disappears, followed by laughter. *A-heh-heh-heh-heh-heh.*

Doors start slamming. People come outside to investigate. They stare at me, faces stone masks. Those looks are asking questions.

Who is that strange boy?

Is he an outsider?

Why's he making all that noise?

Should we call Chief Beaumont?

I wave at the lookers. "It's okay. I'm walking dogs for Mr. P, Mrs. Callahan, and Professor Muller. Chief Beaumont gave me permission."

Hearing familiar names seems to work. The people go back

to their air-conditioned houses and big-screen TVs. I untangle leashes and check dogs. All four are covered in dried grass and dirt. Baby's ear ribbons have come loose. I retie them in a double knot. Siegfried whines, holding a front paw in the air.

"Good dog, Siegfried." My voice calm, the way Beth does when she treats our animals, I examine his foot. A sliver of wood is stuck in the pad. Gently, I ease it out. He whines but lets me wash his foot with water. I give him a drink and refill the jar lid for the other three. While they're drinking, I dry off Siegfried's hurt paw with the tail of my T-shirt and examine it more closely.

"It's not too bad, Siegfried. A little antiseptic soap and warm water, and it will be just fine."

Which means I have to tell Professor Muller what happened.

As I'm working with Siegfried, Apollo finishes his business. I tie a fourth bag to a belt loop. A Farm-&-Fleet logo, more bouncing peanuts. My job done for the day, I use my hands to brush off the dogs and finish the route.

Dropping off Apollo first, I pocket a five-dollar bill.

"Wait, I make Greek sugar cookies for us." Mr. P's house smells like a bakery. "You come in. We eat."

"Um, better not. I have to take the other dogs home."

"Oh, sure, sure." He glances at Buddy, Baby, and Siegfried, picks up Apollo. "Why they all so dirty?" he says, looking at me.

"The, uh, the grass is really dry. Passing cars stirred up dust, too."

A half-lie?

"Oh, sure, sure. I am watering my plants every day." He sets Apollo down and tells me to wait. He returns with a sandwich bag stuffed full of sugar cookies. "For the way home."

"Thanks. That'll be great." We exchange cookies and a bag of peanut-size dog poop.

Mrs. Callahan's house is next. I tie up Apollo on the porch, then take the two peekapoos inside. I'll drop off her house key at the office on my way out.

Professor Muller is the last stop. As we near his house, I see him on the front step, waiting. I notice he's looking at Siegfried, so I look, too.

The dog is limping.

Professor Muller watches as I wash Siegfried's paw with antiseptic soap, listens as I explain what happened. We're standing in his bathroom, Siegfried on the counter.

"My sister taught me how to do this. I'm really sorry it happened."

"Can you identify the boy?" He's stiff backed, stern looking. An unhappy professor of medieval mythological studies getting ready to fail a student. "It appears you were injured, too." He indicates scrapes on my knees I hadn't noticed.

I try to swallow, but my mouth is so dry, I can't make spit. I used all my water on the dogs.

"It all happened so fast...." I cop out on the truth, afraid if he learns Justin has it in for me, my dog-walking days will be over. "But I hear that Chief Beaumont won't take the word of a kid. He has to catch someone in the act before he'll do anything."

A guttural sound comes out of the professor's throat. "I cannot have Siegfried put in danger. Do you understand what I'm saying, Samuel?" He hands me five dollars.

That's it. I failed the test. He's telling me I can't walk his dog anymore.

I pocket the five and lift Siegfried down from the bathroom counter. When I set him on the floor, his stumpy tail wags like crazy.

"But see, Siegfried had a good time. And the exercise was good for him. It probably won't happen again. I think it was just an accident...."

I'm running my mouth intentionally. My grandpa always said *The squeaky wheel gets the grease*.

"Please..." And whining seems to work for Rosie. "Remember, you just had surgery."

Professor Muller's mask softens. "Well, it *is* important that

Siegfried gets exercise." Another raspy sigh. "We will try it one more time, see if it happens again. If it does..."

This time, I don't have to wonder what he's telling me. If Justin runs me off the road again, I won't be walking Siegfried anymore. Or the other dogs, either. Professor Muller will tell Mrs. Callahan and Mr. P what happened, and I won't have a job at all. Which means I won't get my puppy.

Justin will win, and give me the loser sign.

Again.

Chapter 16

The next day, Yee and Anise bike over to Bailey's for cheerleading practice. For once, all three are being themselves. Just girls having fun, not what others expect them to be. I sit on the front porch with Sid and George, and Rosie holds Blondie, Bailey's long-tailed mixed cocker. We all watch as they practice a pyramid cheer.

"Bubble gum, bubble gum,
Pop, pop.
Bubble gum, bubble gum,
Pop, pop.
Our team, our team,
On top.
Your team, your team,
Ker-PLOP."

When they get to the "on top" part, Anise and Bailey stand to one side, one leg bent for Yee to stand on. Yee can climb up and stay balanced as long as she holds their hands. But at "Ker-plop," when she turns loose to stretch tall, the pyramid starts to wobble. When Bailey and Anise's legs turn to jelly, the pyramid becomes the leaning tower of Pisa. Then a heap of rubble on the ground.

Everyone laughs. But I'm bummed.

Yesterday, I ended up in a similar heap that could cost me my job. Thanks to Justin. I earned fifteen dollars on my first day of work. If I deduct the ten dollars the ad cost, I now have a hundred and five dollars saved. A long way from three hundred and fifty.

The cheerleading squad takes a break, and we sit around talking and drinking cold pop. We're all dressed for the heat: T-shirts, shorts, and tennis shoes. Except Sid. He's wearing khaki shorts, a shirt with a collar, and sandals. When they become curious about my scraped knees, I tell them how Justin ran me and the dogs off the road.

"I despise him." Anise looks angry. "He's such a bully."

Rosie says, "What's a bully?"

"Someone who enjoys tormenting and intimidating others," Sid tells her. "Justin does seem to enjoy that a good deal."

"He calls me Fatso." Bailey's smile takes a nose dive. "I hate him, too."

"Patty says he's a sissy," Rosie says. Justin's little sister, Patty, is in her class at school. "She told me her daddy gets real mad at him 'cause he won't walk Bruno. She says it's 'cause he's afraid of him."

"He's afraid of his own dog?" I can't imagine such a thing.

Anise looks at Yee. "You think that's why he never lets Bruno out of his cage?"

Yee shrugs.

"Patty's in the pageant with me. She's doing a dance, too. Want to see mine?" Without waiting for an answer, Rosie starts stomping in a circle and making grunting sounds.

Neanderthal man, getting ready to hunt mastodons.

"Let's try it this way. I learned how to do this in my modern dance class in the burbs." Anise spins in circles, looking graceful and elegant. Everyone claps when she finishes.

Rosie tries to imitate her. Anise says she has a natural talent for dance and asks Rosie if she would like her to be her choreographer.

"What's that?" asks Rosie.

"A choreographer is sort of a teacher. A *dance* teacher. If you want, I'll come up with a modern Chippewa dance. A Chippewa warrior priestess ballet."

"*Cool.* I always wanted to be a warrior priestess."

Girls. I shake my head and sigh, hear Sid sigh, too.

"And if you want, I could do your hair." Yee slips the rubber band off Rosie's ponytail and combs through it with her fingers. "I have a conditioner that will make it shiny. And we can braid it, like a real priestess."

Rosie agrees in a heartbeat. Who wouldn't? Yee has the prettiest hair in school.

"I need to take care of something. Would one of you watch Rosie when she crosses the road?"

"I'll make sure she gets home...." Sid pauses, looking at me. "We need to talk about the pageant."

Sid's look tells me that today's the day he's going to warn Rosie she's not a shoo-in to win the pageant. That there's no need for a third costume.

"Maybe Bailey can bring Yee and Anise over to see the new, clean Max when they finish practice," he says.

"Yeah. You gotta see Max. He turned into a..." Rosie hesitates, looking at Sid.

"Boo-sha-peer." He pronounces it slowly.

I groan. "I'll tell you what he is—I'll even spell it for you. He's a *D-O-G.*"

Sid looks at me. "Yes, a Boo-sha-peer is a dog, just as a golden retriever, a Labrador, and a German shepherd are dogs. Also peekapoos, poodles, Pekingese, Chihuahuas—"

"We get it, Sid!" Yee covers her ears with her hands.

"We'll come over soon as we finish practice," Bailey says. She puts Blondie in the backyard so practice can resume.

Rosie now has a clothes designer, a choreographer, and a hairstylist, and Sid is going to straighten things out about costumes. Which means there will be tears later. But I'm cool with tears because I'm getting free babysitting out of the deal. Time enough to make a phone call.

Alone in the house, I hurry to the living room. Dialing quickly, I get an immediate answer.

"Kendall's Kennels. This is Alice Kendall."

"This is Sam Smith again. I called you about the puppies for sale. Do you still have them?"

"I remember you. And yes, I have two males and the female left. Sold one of the males yesterday." A pause on the line. "So, you have the money now?"

"Not exactly, but I'll have it soon. I just wanted to let you know that I will *definitely* be buying one of the males." I listen to Mrs. Kendall clear her throat.

"Like I told you, Sam. This is a business. I can't hold a dog—"

"Yes, ma'am, I know. I was just checking to make sure you still had one. I'll call you soon, but it won't be long now. Just a few weeks. Okay?" Another pause.

"Well, you can call back, but you must understand that I can't make any guarantees."

"Yes, ma'am, I understand all about business. I'll call you back soon."

I hang up, pumped. If I'm a squeaky wheel with Mrs. Kendall, I just know she'll give in and hold a puppy for me.

Giggles tell me the cheerleading squad is on its way to see Max, so I hurry to catch up. Rosie is sitting on the ground next to Sid, watching George race around the wading pool like he's in the Indy 500. I don't see a single tear staining Rosie's cheeks.

"I can't believe it's the same dog," Yee says, giving Max a good rub on his sides. He eats it up.

"Me either." Anise takes care of the head rubbing. "But he could stand some mouthwash." Her mouth puckers like she's been eating a lemon.

"Beth brought home some dog biscuits, the ones with charcoal that help bad breath. I, uh, I just haven't had time to give him any."

"Well, go get them." Yee looks at me, hands on hips.

I leave, sighing.

When I return, everyone takes turns feeding Max. With all the noise, Birdie flies off the nest.

Anise moans, "Oh, no, we made her abandon the eggs."

"Naw. She'll be back soon as we leave. She sits for thirty or forty minutes, then takes a break to eat and exercise. It's normal."

"Yeah," Rosie says. "Max stands guard while she's gone. They're married now, and he's adopted the eggs."

Everyone laughs. Except me.

Suddenly, Sid points at the nest. "Look, Sam. I believe that egg is hatching."

Everyone crowds close, looking at a crack in one of the small blue eggs.

"Birdie must have been sitting longer than we thought. Beth told me it takes ten to fourteen days for the eggs to hatch."

"I want to watch the eggs get born." Rosie pushes closer.

I pull her away. "You need to give it some space. It takes a long time for the chick to get out. And they hatch in the order Birdie laid them, so she still needs to keep the others warm."

"Max is an excellent bird herder." Sid puts George into his cage. "And I must be a gerbil herder now. It's time for me to go home."

"Me too." Yee gets up to leave.

Anise gets up, too.

Bailey leads Rosie and the other cheerleaders toward the road.

As I retrieve a half-empty bag of dog biscuits from the ground, Max runs up, begging for another. "Your breath *would* stop a train." I toss him a biscuit. He catches it between his teeth and wags his tail.

"Walk me to the road, Sam?" Sid is standing behind me.

I turn to look at him. "Hey, thanks for telling Rosie she's not a shoo-in for the contest. She handle it okay?"

"She understood perfectly ... I think." Sid's shoulders droop. "I won't be coming back for a while, Sam. My mother has decided to paint the conference room pink."

"Pink?"

He shrugs. "It's a princess contest. Princesses like pink. So I have now been given the job of room painter."

"That's too bad. But there'll be plenty of summer left after it's over."

He grins. "Yes, that is true."

"And I'll be getting my new puppy before long."

"Maybe we can have a party to welcome it. A naming party."

"*Splendid* idea. Something important sounding. Like Bruno."

"Bruno?" He frowns. "Isn't that's the name of Justin's dog?"

"Yeah. I want my puppy to be named after a mythological god, too. You know, something impressive."

He nods, looking thoughtful. "You mean like George. Many kings have been named George."

"Yeah, *exactly*. Like *King* George the Gerbil."

Sid gives me a knuckle bump. "Will I see you at the pageant?"

I hadn't considered going to the Princess Pageant. He picks up on it.

"Your sister will be very disappointed if you don't come."

"Yeah … yeah, I should probably be there."

"Good." He grins as he pushes off. "You can sit with King George and me. It will be fun."

"Fun." I say the word, but I don't mean it. Even though Sid has explained the rules to Rosie, I know she's not prepared to lose. There will be nothing but tears and temper tantrums on pageant day.

Chapter 17

I wake up with a headache on Friday morning because I had bad dreams. I change out of my sleeping clothes and walk downstairs. Rosie's at the kitchen table, sitting in front of a bowl of Cheerios, but she's too excited to eat. Her legs swing like opposing pendulums as she rattles on about the new dance Anise is teaching her. A caution light starts to blink behind my eyes.

"You still may not win the talent show, Rosie. Justin said Patty's been taking dance since she was three years old."

"I know, Sid explained all that to me." She's wearing a purple tank top over a luminous lime-green skort. "The judges will pick who they think is best." She looks at me, eyes serious. "I'm going to practice real hard."

Rats. She still thinks she could win.

"Yeah, well, Patty's mother will probably buy her expensive costumes, too. You still might not win. That means you won't get a tiara."

"That's what Patty said."

"Patty? Justin's sister told you she was going to win the tiara?"

"Yeah, she's a bully, too. Yee told me that bullies pick on you to make you afraid of them so you won't try. She said the best thing to do is ignore them. So that's what I'm doing. I'm ignoring Patty." Rosie pauses at the door. "I really like your friends, Sammy. They're the nicest."

Yeah, they *are* the nicest.

I leave for work, a larger water bottle clipped to a belt loop. A ball cap in my hip pocket for shade. A bigger jar lid stuffed in the other pocket for a water dish. I considered bringing bent nails to throw on the road to puncture Justin's tires but decided against it. If I gave other people flat tires, Chief Beaumont would toss me out like he was throwing a touchdown pass.

CountryWood: 6. Sam Smith: 0. Game over.

I coast down the driveway, remembering my dreams. Not dreams, nightmares. Justin forcing me into the ditch. Running over the dogs. Making the *L* sign on his forehead.

Maybe he won't bother me today....

I meet Bailey at the road. She smiles as we pass each other. I muster a smile, too. Plastic.

Bertha's at the security gate, grinning as she hands me an orange pass. "Morning, Sam."

Hearing my name, Chief Beaumont walks outside. "How you doin', Sam?"

He stands in front of me. Legs spread wide and arms crossed like a linebacker. A *determined* linebacker.

"Um, fine." I wait. More is coming.

"Had reports of a disturbance Wednesday, 'bout the time you were walking the dogs. Loud engine, dogs barking. You hear any such thing?"

He's going to give me a citation for disturbing the peace.

Take away my gate privileges.

Toss me out like a football.

"I, uh, I might've heard something...but four dogs keep me pretty busy." A lie, of course, and the look on the chief's face says he knows it. I duck my head and look at my watch. "I, uh, I have to pick up the key from Mrs. Callahan."

He waves me through the gate. I hurry to the office, resisting looking back. I watch a lot of cop shows on TV. Liars always look over their shoulder.

It only takes ten minutes to round up the dogs because Mr. P, Mrs. Callahan, and Professor Muller live so close to each other.

I'm glad to see that all four dogs have recovered from Justin's terror attack. And even happier that Siegfried isn't limping anymore.

I keep an eye on the rear and listen for a gasoline-powered engine, but it's smooth sailing. I've just tied the fourth plastic bag to my belt when I hear the sound. I spin around but see nothing. Siegfried nudges my leg, alerting me that I need to rotate a hundred eighty degrees. I turn to see a muscle shirt leaning over the windshield of a golf cart. Justin's conducting a frontal attack today.

I pick up the smaller dogs and take off. Siegfried races beside me. When Justin spins in a tight circle, I spot a wide gap between two houses. It's against orders to leave the designated path, but only one thought fills my mind. Survival. Mine and the dogs'.

I stop on the other side of the gap. A six-foot-tall white PVC fence confronts me. L-shaped. One of the inside corners of Country-Wood. A dead end.

I spit on the ground and say, "Crap."

I consider my options. I can't go back because Justin's there. There's no easy way to get the dogs over a six-foot fence. And there's no use trying to hide because Justin knows every inch of this place.

And then it hits me. It's not just a dead end. It's a minefield for golf carts. Big trees. Thorny raspberry bushes. Rough ungraded ground. Lots of boulders.

"*Run,* Siegfried." We make it into the trees and the boulder field just as Justin roars through the gap. He slams on his brakes, squealing to a stop.

"*Chicken!* You gotta come out of there sooner or later, and I got all day."

Swell. Another plan that wasn't foolproof. Justin might have all day, but I don't. I wish for a miracle.

Barely a minute passes before Justin turns his golf cart around. I watch as he roars away.

It's the miracle I hoped for. But what caused it?

I turn, expecting to see fluorescent halos. Instead, I see flashing lights on a patrol car. Chief Beaumont steps out. Legs spread wide. Arms crossed.

Aww, man.

Siegfried follows behind as I carry Apollo, Buddy, and Baby to the car.

"Believe you're off your path, Sam. And you're supposed to be walking dogs, not carrying them." His probing eyes do exploratory surgery. "Got an explanation for that?"

"Um, yeah, uh..." I stammer a lot, hoping to buy time. My mind floats somewhere between righteous truth and flat-out lie. "See, I discovered this place by accident, and it's a great place to walk dogs. You know, away from the traffic...and people's houses...and things that scare them."

"Things that scare them..." He looks down the road where Justin disappeared. "You hear a loud engine a few minutes ago? Like maybe a gasoline-powered golf cart?"

I attempt to swallow, but my mouth has grown hair. "Maybe," I wheeze.

He pauses. "Can't help you if you don't help me, Sam. Was it Justin?"

Time passes. He stares at me.

"I, uh, I really need this job." I stare at the ground.

"Uh-huh," he says again, nodding thoughtfully. "I think you just confirmed what I already knew." He turns his attention to the rocky place behind me. "Problem with this lot is it's in the corner of the development where no decent road could be built. Or houses, for that matter. There's been talk about making a walking path to it, turning it into a park." He pauses, rubbing his mouth. "Would make a good place to walk dogs, wouldn't it?"

"Yes, sir, a real good place."

"The dogs done with their business?"

"Yes, sir."

"Get in, then." He motions me toward the backseat of his cruiser. "I'll take you and the dogs home, they've gotten enough exercise. On the way, we'll talk about changing your route to come here instead. I'll explain everything to the dogs' owners. That way, neither you nor their owners have to worry about their dogs getting injured again."

Again. He knows about Siegfried getting hurt.

He looks at me. "That okay with you?"

I wheeze, "Yes, sir. That is *very* okay with me."

Chief Beaumont's dark face turns darker. "And then I'm going to have a talk with a certain someone's father about taking away his son's driving privileges."

Justin. He's talking about Justin.

Woohoo! Home free now. No more bad dreams. No more hurt dogs.

And Justin the Jerk will be the big loser.

Chapter 18

It's just Rosie and me for breakfast on Sunday morning. Beth left early to run errands, and Mom had to deliver plants to a local church. "The parishioners volunteered to help plant them before services begin," she told me as she left. "And I never turn down free help. Which is why I appreciate you so much, Sammy. Oh, and I left a list of things I could use your help with in the garden shed. Those raccoons paid us another visit."

"I'm going over to Bailey's." Rosie wipes her mouth with her sleeve.

"Not until you've fed the cats—and use your napkin."

"You sound just like Beth."

"It's 'cause I'm the alpha person."

"Huh?"

"Never mind. Finish your cereal before you go."

Rosie drains her cereal bowl and leaves to feed the cats.

I'm alone. The perfect time to be a squeaky wheel again. Mrs. Kendall answers the phone right away, tells me she still has puppies for sale, and gives me the same I-can't-make-you-any-promises talk.

I hang up, feeling good. Plenty of puppies left, and Mrs. Kendall *definitely* knows I want one of them.

After cleaning up the kitchen, I head for the garden shed. Mom's list includes dumping plants the raccoons ruined into the compost pile. Scrubbing the empty pots with disinfectant to kill bacteria. Weeding the perennial garden. After that, I'm to mist the annuals. As she put it in her instruction note, *Annuals can't survive in a desert. But the good news is, rain is in the forecast—lots of it.*

It takes me all morning to finish the list. Stomach rumbling like a volcano about to erupt, I head to the house for lunch. Then I spot Wednesday and Saturday, sneaking toward the barn. Bodies skimming the ground. Ears flat. Tails snapping like whips. Wondering what they're up to, I decide to investigate.

Sneaking up on two sneaky cats isn't easy, unless those two cats are sneaking up on something else. Peeking around the corner of the barn, I see them. Tails twitching. Eyes fixed, staring at the nest. The *empty* nest. Birdie is gone.

I look for Max and hear him snoring. He's in front of the nest, nestled under the evergreen bush. Dead to the world.

As the cats move closer, I hear it. Tiny cheeps. Birdie's eggs are hatching.

"Max—wake up."

Max jumps to his feet. Wednesday and Saturday fade into the shadows. I hurry to the nest and stare at one of the tiniest little birds I've ever seen. And the ugliest. Naked, wet, and blind. The baby robin's wrinkled yellow eyelids cover its eyes completely. Its red mouth is a gaping hole.

Sitting down next to Max, we watch Birdie bring back a long earthworm. She deposits half in the chick's mouth, waits for it to gulp it down, and gives it the other half. Then she's off again for another worm.

I creep close enough to see another egg with a hole in it. The chick inside has broken through the shell with its egg tooth. Beth told me it takes a chick a day to hatch out. Because it gets tired, it has to stop to rest.

"Sammy, I'm hungry!" The yell comes from the back of the house. Rosie is home from Bailey's, yelling at me from the kitchen.

"You take care of your chick," I whisper in Max's ear. "I have one of my own to keep me busy."

Great. Now I'm a sister herder talking to a bird herder.

Max puts a paw on my leg and emits a foul-smelling burp. Rotten eggs and sour milk.

"Okay, okay." I toss him a couple of the dog biscuits that I've started carrying in my pocket.

TV is mostly reruns, so I slip away to my room after supper. Sometimes it's nice to hang out by yourself. No chore list from Mom. No bossy older sister blackmailing you. No whiny baby sister to feed.

Mom's bedroom is on the main floor. Beth's, Rosie's, and mine are upstairs. Our rooms are small, just big enough for a twin bed, a chest, and small desk. My room is at the back of the house where there's not much noise from traffic. Quiet.

In the summer, I push my bed under the window to get the cool night air. Tonight there's a good breeze blowing. The inky darkness outside the window makes the room seem even quieter.

I pull out my dog book. Turn pages. Stop at the section for German shepherds. Stare at pictures of dark regal-looking dogs.

"Rin Tin Tin," I whisper, thinking of names for the puppy. "No, Rin Tin Tin's been used." I try out Shadow and Eclipse and shake my head. Too tame for a regal dog.

I lay my scrapbook aside and pick up the book Professor Muller gave me. The book is old. The stiff cover is black fading to gray. The pages are yellowed on the edges. I learn Siegfried was a mythical hero who destroyed a dragon to save a great warrior. The weekday names Tuesday, Wednesday, Thursday, and Friday started out as special days to honor Germanic gods and goddesses. Tuesday came from Tiu, a god of combat. Wednesday from Woden, the Anglo-Saxons' most important god. Thursday was named for Punor, god of thunder. And Friday for Frige, the goddess of beauty.

Images of gigantic muscular figures standing on dark storm clouds, long hair and beards whipping in the wind, fill my mind. I debate telling Rosie the origins of the names she gave her cats but nix the idea. She would really be impossible to live with if I did.

Still, I like the idea of naming the puppy after a mythical god who's bigger than life. I go through my own list of heroes. Superman. Spider-Man. Batman. Iron Man. The Hulk. None of them feel right. Yawning, I close the book. Sid will help me figure it out.

I turn off my reading light and kick back the covers, letting the cool night air envelop me. The chirping noise of crickets rubbing their wings together and frogs belching air through vocal sacs fades to silence.

The noise is low. Rumbling. Like the deep croaking of a giant frog. Flashes of light puncture the darkness, casting shadows across my bed.

I bolt upright. Listening. Remembering Mom's note about rain in the forecast. *Lots of it.* Images flash through my mind like tiny internal bolts of lightning.

Max—

Birdie—

Baby robins—

I race downstairs, bare feet slapping the floor like seal flippers. Picking up the flashlight on the back porch, I run for the barn. In the tossing beam of the light, I see Max peeking around the corner. Fur blowing wildly. Pacing. Forward, toward me. Back toward the nest.

"Max—*come.*" He refuses. I give him the command again. He won't leave Birdie.

Dumb old dog.

I race to the shelf in the garage where we store camping equipment. Grab Beth's one-man tent, the quick-setup kind with a fiberglass frame that folds into a disk. Snatch my old sleeping bag and a hammer on the way out the door.

Thunder, louder. Lightning, cracking. A metallic smell on the wind. Ozone. Nature's electricity. Not just rain, a thunderstorm is coming.

I run faster. As I get closer, I hear Max. Whining.

Setting the flashlight on the ground, I aim the beam at Birdie's nest. BB eyes stare at me. Wings and tail stretch like an umbrella over the nest.

I pop open the tent in front of the evergreen bush, position it so the door is downwind to keep water from blowing inside, stake it down. Unzipping the front flap, I unroll the sleeping bag so it's flat. A wall-to-wall carpet inside the tent, flannel side up. The perfect doggie bed.

"Inside, Max." I point to the tent opening. He doesn't move. I can see him in the lightning flashes. Muzzle studded with raindrops. Hair blowing. Panic in his chestnut-colored eyes. I give the command again. Nothing.

What's wrong? I'm the alpha person.

Raindrops pepper my neck and head. I give the command again.

Max becomes the Hulk. Unmovable.

There's a bolt of lightning, a crash of thunder. Simultaneous. The storm is on top of us.

Grabbing Max's collar, I pull him into the tent and zip the door. The air crackles. Rain pelts down. Thunder shakes the ground. Max tries to push through the door, but I pull him down next to me and start talking. Low and calm.

"She's all right, Max. Birds have been weathering storms for hundreds of years. *Thousands* of years. That's how they survived this long."

He settles down but still trembles. We listen to deafening peals of thunder. Blink at blinding flashes of lightning. Watch the tent sag under the weight of water. In my mind's eye, I see mythological gods battling fire-breathing dragons. Thunder, the dragon's roar. Lightning bolts, clashing swords. The storm gods retreat in time, and the downpour wimps to a steady rain.

Mom's going to be so happy....

Unzipping the tent opening a slit, I shine the light toward Birdie. She's a little black lump, wings and tail drooping over the sides of her nest. Intact.

"See, Max, I told you she'd be okay. I know these things 'cause I'm the alpha person." Max pants, exuding a putrid smell. Old banana peels and rotten turnips. I regret not bringing charcoal dog biscuits.

Decision time. Get drenched going back to the house? Or weather the rest of the night in the tent?

I stretch out. Sleeping bag a mattress.

A loud explosion comes from Max's direction and a noxious odor fills the tent.

"Aww, man." I pull a corner of blue-plaid flannel over my nose.

Sleeping bag a gas mask.

Chapter 19

"Sam, wake up." Beth unzips the tent opening.

I follow Max outside, groggy. Birdie is feeding earthworms to three baby birds.

"Look." I point to the nest. "Another egg hatched last night!"

"You spent the night out here, didn't you?"

"Max wouldn't leave Birdie and...well, I thought the tent would help protect the nest."

"A nylon seawall, huh?" Beth smiles. Max always has been terrified of thunderstorms. "Thought you had to work this morning?"

"Yeah, ten o'clock. But I'll take care of Max and Birdie before I leave—*and* take your tent to the garage."

"Don't think Max needs any water, or Birdie, for that matter. Dog dish and birdbath are overflowing. And just leave the tent up for a while, it could rain again." She drags my sleeping bag out of the tent and stretches it over the clothesline to air out. "Think you'll be needing this tonight."

I stare at the flapping sleeping bag. Army brown. Plaid flannel lining, half of it coated with dog hair. A giant moth, drying its wings. "What do you mean?"

"Left your window open. Mattress is soaked. Floor, too."

"*Rats.* Mom mad?"

"*Steamed.* Better drag the mattress out to the picnic table to dry out. Probably take days, even as hot as it is."

"Okay, soon as I take care of Max."

"I've got time to feed him. You get showered and cleaned

up." She pauses, smiling again. "Might want to steer clear of Mom, though. She went looking for you when you didn't come down for breakfast. Wasn't expecting to wade into a swimming pool."

"Great. Just great. I'll never get out of the doghouse for this one."

"You might just be right." Her laughter rings across the yard. "Go on, I'll run interference for you. She's on the phone with a customer, so it's a good chance to slip in unnoticed."

Big sisters are great.

As I walk to the house, it hits me. Soon, Beth won't be here, bossing me around. Or blackmailing me. Or running interference when Mom busts my chops. She'll be gone. Gone for good.

All at once, a big hole opens up in my chest.

Chapter 20

I know things have changed as soon as I pull up to the security gate. Bertha doesn't smile when she hands me my pass. Chief Beaumont isn't smiling, either.

"Vandals struck again," he says.

His mouth is a straight ruler. A rigid strip. His shirt wet under the armpits. The sweet-sour tang of sweat fills my nose, and I wonder if I'm smelling his sweat...or mine.

"Solar lights along *certain* driveways destroyed," he says.

Certain driveways? I wait, trying to decipher his code.

"Ripped out of the ground and broken in half. Malicious mischief. Someone with an axe to grind."

Code cracked. He thinks I did it.

"I didn't do it—honest."

"Don't think you did, Sam, but others..."

"Oh. Because I'm an outsider."

"Explained to everyone affected that you wouldn't jeopardize your job that way...." He pauses. "But the vandalism occurred along the route you take, and..." Another pause.

Is he telling me he's firing me?

"Justin's father was so angry when he learned how Justin was acting with you, he's making him walk Bruno every day."

I crunch his words, searching for the important piece. "So you're saying Justin did it to get even with me?"

"But can't prove it. Dark night. Kid was laughing—that's what woke the people up—but they couldn't identify him." He looks away, then settles his face on mine. Eyes narrow, like if he's measuring me.

There's more coming....

"When I questioned some of the kids, they said you bragged on the bus about climbing over the fence."

I am dead. A corpse. Roadkill.

"But I didn't mean it. I was just joking around. Ask Yee and Anise, they'll tell you."

"Already did," he says. "They said the same thing."

My heart throbs in my temples. "What do I do now, Chief Beaumont?"

"Go about your job as usual. Most times, these things blow over...." He looks me in the eyes. "But be on your best behavior. Word gets around fast here. People will be watching you like a bug under a microscope."

When I pick up the house key from Mrs. Callahan, I ask if her place was vandalized.

"No." She stares at me, not smiling. "Nor was Mr. P's or Mr. Muller's." She hesitates as she places the key in my hand.

I bike toward Mr. P's house, legs stumps that won't bend. People work in their front yards, replacing solar lights, sweeping glass shards and metal strips into piles. They stop to stare when I pass. Their looks say the same thing. *There he is. That outsider who climbed over the fence and did this terrible thing.*

I spot a familiar vehicle in one of the driveways. Mom's van. As I bike past, she yells, "Hi, Sammy! See you at home later today." The people on the street turn their icy stares on her. My stomach drops.

If they know I'm her son, will they stop having her do work for them?

Mr. P's place wasn't vandalized, but he isn't smiling, either. Worse, he looks at me the same way Mrs. Callahan did. Which doesn't make sense. But I know a person who can explain it.

I tie leashes to the porch post at Professor Muller's house. He sits on the front step with me, bad leg stuck out stiff in front of him, and listens as I tell how Mr. P and Mrs. Callahan are acting.

"It's like they're mad at me 'cause Justin *didn't* vandalize their places. Which doesn't add up—none of it adds up." I pull fuzzy fiber off my jean cutoffs, flick it in the air, watch it float away. Man-made pollen. "I mean, if Justin was trying to get back at me, wouldn't he hit their places instead of the other ones? And yours, too?"

"*Ahh*...a red herring." His fingers make a tent. His eyebrows arch like a steeple. "Do you know what that is, Samuel?"

"Well, a herring's a fish, so I guess a red herring would be a *red* fish."

"A *smelly* red fish. Criminals in olden times would throw a red herring on the ground so bloodhounds couldn't follow them."

"Um, o-*kay*..."

His lungs turn to air bellows, pumping out a sigh. "The scent would throw the dogs off the trail."

I stare at him.

Another ragged sigh escapes. "It would have been too obvious to vandalize our places, as we are the ones who hired you," he says. "So striking at others is intended to mislead the authorities. And because we were spared, our neighbors would think you didn't do damage to our property because we are your... benefactors."

"No...Justin wouldn't be that smart. Would he?"

Bony shoulders lift in unison. "You know him better than I do, Samuel. What do *you* think?"

"Well, he's a big gamer...."

His head swivels so he can look at me, yellowed eyes asking questions.

"You know, he likes to play games on his Xbox."

"Games of strategy?"

"Yes, sir. Games where you beat the socks off the enemy."

No, kill the enemy. And in this game Justin wants to *kaput* me.

"Should I apologize to everybody whose places were damaged, Professor Muller? Would that make it okay?"

He pauses, blinking rhythmically. "No, just continue as

Chief Beaumont told you to do. These things have a way of quieting down, *but*—" A frown cracks his forehead. "In all likelihood, Justin expected you to be fired and you weren't, so who's to say what he might try? As John Milton said, 'He that studieth revenge keepeth his own wounds green, which otherwise would heal and do well.'"

Even though the words are cryptic, the warning is clear. *Watch out.*

My muscles are bricks as I start out with the dogs. My intestines are stringy knots. Although Justin's driving privileges have been taken away, I watch over my shoulder. Rules don't mean anything to him. When we reach the corner lot and nothing has happened, my muscles relax.

I turn the four dogs loose so they can run free, leashes still attached so I can catch them easily. As I watch them play, I hear a noise behind me. Glancing toward the gap between houses, I see a boy and a dog watching us. Not just any dog. The most beautiful sable German shepherd I've ever seen. The dog of my dreams.

A giant, the shepherd must weigh a hundred pounds. His coat is the color of ebony. The silver hair on his back, moonlight. His teeth, long and razor sharp. I can tell because the dog is lunging at his leash. Snarling and snapping.

Bruno the Beast.

Justin stumbles toward me. A pull toy dragged by a mythological warrior dog.

My muscles tighten to bricks again.

"*Come*, Siegfried. Apollo, Buddy, Baby—*come*." I grab their leashes. Glance at Bruno. He's close enough now that I can see yellow strings of drool.

"Heel, Bruno!" Justin yells. "Heel!" His commands are useless. Straws in a tornado.

My heart pounds in my ears. My breath catches in my throat. My mind fills with images. Bruno snapping Apollo in half like a snack cracker. Cracking Buddy and Baby like chicken bones. Gobbling Siegfried for dessert. I chance another look.

Justin's face is worse than Bruno's. Twisted. Bloodred. Angry. I wonder what he intends to do. And how to stop him before he can do it.

Stall, the voice in my head whispers.

"Gee, Bruno's a beautiful dog, Justin." I hear my voice shaking and hope Justin can't.

"Yeah, thought you'd like to see what a *real* dog looks like." He lets out a hyena laugh.

What was it Rosie said?

Ignore bullies....

"Heel, Siegfried." The little Min Pin falls into step. I pick up Apollo, Buddy, and Baby and focus on ignoring Justin and Bruno. Legs trembling, I mumble, "Um, gotta get the dogs home. If I'm late, their owners come looking for me."

The lie is as thin as my voice. I try to hurry, but my muscles have turned to wet noodles.

Reaching the road, I chance another peek and can't believe my eyes. Justin is on the ground, yelling "Heel!" again and again. Bruno has become a four-legged Determinator, dragging him like a floppy toy. In desperation, Justin loops Bruno's leash around a tree to stop him. A dog hitching post.

That's when I get it. I don't have to ignore Justin the Jerk. The bully can't do anything to me because he has his hands full with another bully. Bruno.

Time for a taste of his own medicine....

"Hey, Justin. I got a book on dog training, you want to borrow it? Even a *pedigreed* dog's not worth anything if it can't be trained." I throw in a hyena giggle. *A-heh-heh-heh-heh-heh.*

The last words I hear are icing on the cake: "Heel, Bruno. *Please,* heel!"

I deliver Apollo to Mr. P and tell him everything went fine. He gives me five dollars, plus cookies. Buddy and Baby are next. When they're locked safely inside, I jog with Siegfried to his house, pick up the backyard, and get another five dollars. I turn to leave, but Professor Muller stops me.

"Have you read the book on mythology?"

"Yes, sir, some of it. The days of the week were named for heroes. Like Tuesday, Wednesday, Thursday, and Friday."

His dark eyes shine.

"And I read all about Siegfried."

He smiles.

"But I couldn't find a hero or a god named Bruno."

"Bruno?" The pleased look changes to puzzled.

"Justin Wysocki named his German shepherd Bruno. I figure it's for one of the mythological heroes."

"I'm afraid not, Samuel. *Bruno* is German for brown."

"Brown. You mean, like the *color* brown?"

He nods.

"So it's like naming a dog Brownie?"

"That would be a fair translation."

Justin's big expensive dog with a pedigree a yard long is named Brownie.

"You're probably thinking of Fenrir," he says.

"Who's that?"

"A giant wolf in myth that, it was foretold, would kill Odin. But others prevented it from doing so. It was killed eventually."

"Yeah?"

"But not before biting off another god's hand."

"Wow, that sucks. But let me get this straight. *Bruno* means…"

"Brown."

I drop off Mrs. Callahan's key at the office and grin all the way home.

Neither Beth nor Mom is smiling. Their faces are flushed; their eyes throw darts at each other. I can tell they've been arguing, but they clam up as soon as I walk into the kitchen.

After Mom stalks out to the garden shed, I turn to Beth. "What's up?"

Beth pours us both a glass of tea from the refrigerator. "Got a flat on my Subaru, and the spare is flat, too. Asked to borrow Mom's van but she has a delivery to make—*had* a delivery to make. She's going to call and see if the customer can pick it up so I can take the van." She takes a long drink, then sighs. "She's insisting I get new tires before I leave for Colorado."

I give it a minute. Say, "Probably a good idea."

Beth turns flashing eyes on me. "Like I told you, I'm *busted*. I've paid my tuition in advance and still have to buy gasoline for the trip. Hopefully, there's some left over for Top Ramen noodles and a bag of apples when I reach Colorado."

"You could talk to Mom about pulling Rosie out of the princess pageant." I take a long drink of tea, letting her consider the option. "That way, she wouldn't have to pay the rest of the entry fee. Seventy-five bucks would go a long way."

Beth answers with silence.

Right. It was a dumb idea.

Chapter 21

Rosie's a superball as we cross the road Tuesday to cheerleading practice. Bouncy. Wound up. "Can I sleep in the tent with you and Max tonight?"

"No. I'm sleeping there because my mattress is wet. Yours isn't."

She darkens to a storm cloud. Ready to pour.

"There's not enough room, and . . ." I take a time-out, searching for something more convincing. Something she'll buy. "And you need your beauty sleep. You know, for the pageant."

"Oh, yeah."

We sit on the front porch, watching Bailey, Yee, and Anise build pyramids. After ten perfect ones, they take a break.

"That's really good, guys. Practice is paying off."

"We've been practicing a lot at camp, too." Bailey's shirt and shorts are starting to bag, a sign her diet is working. "The coach says we're a good team."

"True dat," Anise says. "I heard she's planning on letting us team up after school starts."

"*True dat?*" Bailey looks at Anise.

"Whoops—I slipped. It's something Saffron used to say. You know, street talk. Dad doesn't want me talking like her."

"*True dat.* I like it."

Yee frowns. "It's not proper English." She watches Bailey and Anise roll their eyes at each other. "But it *is* kind of cool."

Yee looks at me. "Speaking of proper English, where's Sid the Brain Kid?"

"It's the pageant. His mom's having him paint the conference room pink."

Talk moves to favorite colors. Pink ranks high.

I yawn.

Talk moves to the pageant.

I get up, walk toward the road.

"Hey, where you going?" Bailey calls out to me.

"Need to take care of chores. Could one of you make sure Rosie gets across the road?"

A chorus of okays trails after me. I don't really have chores. I'm just bored silly with pageant talk.

The house is quiet, too quiet. I start thinking about the puppies. And wondering if they're still available.

I shouldn't bother Mrs. Kendall again....

I dial from Mom's phone in the living room.

"Sold the female puppy just this morning. That leaves two male puppies." Mrs. Kendall hesitates. "You still working to save money?"

"Oh, yes, ma'am. For sure. It's as good as in the bank. I'll be calling you soon." *Click.*

Please, don't let that be a lie.

Chapter 22

Wednesday feels like a spring day. Cool and breezy. The dogs run ahead of me, playing and nipping at each other. I've only had to give them water once. They finish their business fast. I keep a close watch for Justin, but he's a no-show. We're heading back when I see him coming.

Not Justin. Bruno. Running free. No leash.

On purpose?

I gather the three smallest dogs and yell, "Run!" to Siegfried. But Bruno has an edge. Long legs and massive muscles. He topples us like bowling pins. The three little dogs land on top of me, and Siegfried ends up under all of us. Squashed like an aluminum pop can. His cries tell me he's hurt again.

"Get away! Get back! Go home!" I wave my arms at Bruno and stretch them overhead to look bigger. Finally, he retreats. Chief Beaumont pulls up as I'm sorting dogs and helps me untangle leashes. Together we examine Siegfried.

"Just scared, mostly." The little pinscher trembles so badly, he can't stand.

"Justin responsible for this?"

"No, sir. Bruno."

Chief Beaumont frowns. "The dog wasn't on leash?"

"No, sir."

"You're sure it was Bruno?"

"Oh, yeah. Justin walked him on Monday and brought him here to show me. I made fun of him 'cause he couldn't make Bruno mind."

"Made fun of him…," the chief repeats slowly.

The voice in my head says, *Should have ignored him.*

"Yeah," I say. "That probably wasn't a good idea."

Nodding, Chief Beaumont says, "Well, you won't have to worry about that kind of thing anymore."

"What do you mean?"

Is he going to take Bruno away from Justin? Can he do that?

"That's why I came looking for you, Sam. I thought some more about turning the corner lot into a dog park and got approval from the Board of Directors. Soon as I recruit enough volunteers, we'll extend the fenced area. From now on, people can exercise their dogs without fear of getting run over. By car or animal."

"That's *great*. Now Mr. P, Mrs. Callahan, and Professor Muller can exercise their dogs."

"Yes, but…" The chief's look is piercing. "Sam, do you understand what this means?"

"Oh." A vise squeezes my lungs so tight, I can hardly breathe. "I don't have a job anymore, do I?"

"That would be up to the people you're working for. You *could* continue to work until we get the dog run fenced, but…" He looks at Siegfried. "Not sure that's a good idea. I can give Justin's father a citation for letting Bruno run free, but I'm powerless to do much else. If Justin pulls the same stunt again…"

He's worried one of the dogs will get hurt. *Really* hurt.

"But it's important I walk the dogs as long as I can. I don't have enough to buy my puppy."

"You're buying a puppy…." He looks away, then turns back at me. "All right," he says. "I'm taking your word on this incident, Sam. Something I don't ordinarily do."

"It was Bruno, I know it was."

"All right. Get the dogs home now. I have to go issue someone another citation."

This time, I carry Siegfried and let the other three walk. The little warrior dog has earned a free ride.

My mattress hasn't dried completely, so I'm still sharing the tent with Max. As darkness deepens, my mind becomes a calculator figuring how much more I need. I have the hundred dollars I started with, minus ten for the ad. Another thirty I earned. By the weekend, forty-five more. A hundred sixty-five dollars in all. Less than half of what I need. To earn the balance will take...

Over four weeks!

I bury my head in Max's thick coat. Suddenly, he jerks his head up. Growling. Listening, I hear a *snap* outside the tent.

"What is it?" I strain my eyes through the mosquito-net closing. See nothing.

Max pushes to his feet, nosing the door cover to get out. I unzip it and let him out, climb out behind him. He disappears in the shadows.

I listen for him to bark. Or growl.

Nothing.

Wait...what *is* that?

Something rounds the corner of the barn, tall and flowing. Silvery moonlight gliding across the ground. I wish I'd brought my ball bat from my bedroom. Or that Max were here beside me.

Where *is* Max?

Then I see him. A phantom dog walking beside the apparition.

"Did I wake you, Sammy?"

"Mom—what are you doing out here?"

"I brought your pillow. At least *it's* dry. You know, you could sleep on the sofa in the living room. Be a lot more comfortable."

"No, this is good." I take the pillow. "I, uh, I kind of like listening to the frogs and owls. Besides, Max needs help guarding Birdie."

"All right, then." She shakes her head slightly. "See you in the morning."

Max crawls into the tent with me.

"You could've said something, Max. *I'm* supposed to be your alpha person."

He pants, discharging dog breath. Garlic and spoiled bologna.

I dispense two charcoal dog biscuits.

The night noises seem louder, like the frogs are using amplifiers. The owls, loudspeakers.

Then nothing. A yawning quiet.

The hairs on my arms stand up. Max's ears are at alert. We listen and wait. Wait and listen. Breathing shallow.

Night noises resume.

I sigh, drawing a conclusion. My imagination is working overtime.

Still, a ball bat might come in handy....

As Max starts to snore, I go back to being a calculator. A broken calculator that can't come up with the right number.

Why did I have to mention a dog park to Chief Beaumont?

Sleeping bag a crying towel.

Chapter 23

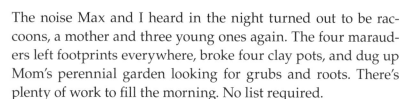

The noise Max and I heard in the night turned out to be raccoons, a mother and three young ones again. The four marauders left footprints everywhere, broke four clay pots, and dug up Mom's perennial garden looking for grubs and roots. There's plenty of work to fill the morning. No list required.

After cheer practice, Bailey, Yee, and Anise come over to visit Max and Birdie. There are four birds now, growing fast. Birdie spends her days pulling worms.

"Poor Birdie, let's help." Rosie runs to the garden shed and brings back shovels. Before I can stop them, she, Anise, and Bailey start digging earthworms. Yee can't stand to touch one, so she brushes Max instead.

"I like that you put up that tent for him. And his breath is a *little* better." She's wearing a pink tank top and tan shorts. "You are feeding him dog biscuits, aren't you?"

"*Yes, ma'am!*" Yee's bossiness grates on my nerves. My sleepless night has made me groggy. My head throbs because I crunched numbers all night. I just want to go to my room and take a nap. But I can't. My mattress is still on the picnic table, drying out.

"Why did you do that?" She looks hurt. "Am I being too bossy?"

I don't answer. I don't want to tell her about seeing ghosts in the night and calculating numbers that wouldn't add up.

"I'll try not to be so bossy."

I make a discovery about girls. Sometimes silence says more than words.

"Did you hear about the dog park? Don't you think it's a great idea?"

Why did she have to bring *that* up?

"Why would I care? I'm an outsider."

She looks hurt again.

I mumble, "Sorry."

"Sammy's going to lose his job." Rosie sits down next to Yee.

"What?" Anise stops shoveling worms. Bailey, too. Everyone stares at Rosie.

"That's what Patty told me today. Her mom bought some plants from Mom."

"Why?" Bailey says, looking at me.

"Oh." Yee's eyes switch to high beams. "It's because we're building a dog park...."

No one says a word with their mouths, but four pairs of eyes give me pitying looks. I can't stand it.

"I, uh, I need to get the trash can out on the street."

"Why?" Bailey frowns. "The trash gets picked up on Fridays. That's tomorrow."

"I know, but I have to work in the morning and won't have time."

A lie and they all know it. There'll be plenty of time in the morning to put out the trash can.

"Empty my trash can, too!" Rosie yells to me.

"Do your own chores!"

The cheerleaders return to Bailey's for practice, and I drag the trash can out to the street. Planning to spend the rest of the day in my room, I hurry back inside. The plan falls apart. I'm drawn to the telephone like a magnet to metal. I dial the number by heart, listen to Mrs. Kendall answer the phone, and ask my usual question.

"As a matter of fact, we sold another one just last night. That leaves just one puppy. A male."

My lungs refuse to inflate. "You...you only have *one* puppy left?"

She confirms the answer and hangs up. *Click.*

I stare at the phone, numb. Can this really be happening?

No, my head insists. There's still time. There aren't enough volunteers to build the dog park. No one will want the last puppy....

Chapter 24

On Friday, I can hardly concentrate when I take the dogs out. Probabilities cloud my thinking.

What are the chances that Mrs. Kendall will sell the last puppy...

That the dog park will be finished before I have enough money saved...

That Justin will turn Bruno loose again...

The last thing on the list is my biggest worry. Citations haven't stopped Justin before.

Dogs have a special insight. They can sense your moods. Like when you're worried. Or nervous. Or scared. Bruno made himself alpha dog because he sensed that Justin was afraid of him. The four little dogs sense my mood today. They're so nervous, they hardly take their eyes off me. Except Siegfried. He looks behind us a lot.

"Let me know if you see anything, Siegfried."

He looks up at me, panting. I don't think it's from the heat.

The traffic is heavier today, with people getting ready for the weekend. BMWs and Volvo station wagons challenge the speed limit. Some going at least forty. Construction people are busy loading equipment on flatbed trailers, massive machines that weigh tons. I hurry the dogs to the corner lot, hoping they'll take care of business quickly.

Relieved when the last doggie bag is tied to a belt loop, I hurry the dogs toward home. When we're a block from Mr. P's house, I let myself relax. Breathe.

All at once, Siegfried pulls to a stop, looking over his shoulder. Turning, I see Justin a half block behind us, holding Bruno's leash. The monster dog is hauling him all over the place, wanting to be free.

Not again—

Old feelings break the surface. Anger. Frustration. I want so bad to make Justin pay.

And then it happens.

Justin lands in the dirt, face-first. An anchor too weak to hold Bruno back. He's a pull toy again.

A disconnected feeling comes over me. Unprompted, words explode out of my mouth.

"Looks like *Brownie* is taking you for another dirt walk, Justin."

Justin sits up and wraps the leash around his waist. A human buoy in a sea of dirt. "His name's *Bruno,* not Brownie."

"Oh, yeah? Well, Professor Muller told me that Bruno means brown in German. That's some fancy name your dog has." My lips make smooching sounds. My mouth says things like "Heel, *Brownie*. Sit, *Brownie*. Good, *Brownie*."

Justin struggles to his feet, glaring. Then I see a slow grin spread across his face...hear the sound of Bruno's leash... unsnapping.

Rats—

"Run, Siegfried!" I pick up Apollo, Buddy, and Baby and take off running, too. A quick look over my shoulder puts wings on my feet. Bruno is bearing down on us like we're petrified rocks. Fossilized stones. Calcified cartilage.

Fenrir, the monster dog of myth, wants to bite the hand off a warrior. That warrior's name? Sammy Smith.

Siegfried's leash rips from my hand, and he races ahead. "Wait for me, Siegfried!" Before I can catch up, Siegfried runs between two cars.

A silver streak passes me, and I make a discovery. I'm not Bruno's target. Siegfried is.

The thudding sound of the construction truck hitting an

object freezes me in my tracks. My heart pounds in my ears. My lungs burn. My legs refuse to move.

The driver jumps out to investigate. Others stop, too. And then Chief Beaumont roars up the street, lights flashing. He hurries over to me.

"I'm sorry. Siegfried pulled the leash out of my hand. I tried to stop him but Bruno was chasing him and—" Tears wash my cheeks.

"Put the dogs in the backseat, Sam."

He opens the door so I can deposit Apollo, Buddy, and Baby inside. I stumble toward the street to pick up what's left of little Siegfried. Suddenly, something pushes against my leg.

"Siegfried?" I pick up the little Min Pin and examine him. "Look, Chief, he's okay. Siegfried's not hurt. But who—"

"Bruno—*Bruno!*"

I race back to Chief Beaumont's car, put Siegfried in the backseat, and run after the chief. At the front of the crowd, I see Justin holding Bruno's head in his lap. Bruno's tongue is hanging loose. His legs are limp. Eyes dulled.

"Let him go, son," Chief Beaumont says to Justin. But Justin won't move.

"Come on, Justin." I kneel next to him and try to pull him away, but he won't let go. "It's no good. Bruno is..." The word sticks in my throat. "He's dead, Justin. Bruno is dead."

"Dead." Justin's voice is thick. Oily. "No, he can't be. Bruno, get up—get up, boy—"

He really loved Bruno....

Suddenly, a man jerks Justin to his feet. "What happened?"

"It was an accident, Dad. He—he got away from me."

"Accident?" Chief Beaumont points to the leash in Justin's hand. "Then why are you carrying *that,* Justin?"

Justin stares at the empty leash, then spins around and points at me. "It was Sammy's fault. He—he was teasing Bruno."

Everyone looks at me, including Chief Beaumont.

"You turned him loose again, didn't you?" Mr. Wysocki

grabs Justin by the shoulder and shoves him toward the street. "Get home, I'll deal with you later."

"Ease up, Wysocki. Your son just lost his dog—"

"Which he parked in the basement along with his other toys." Mr. Wysocki turns to look at Justin. "That's the last dog you'll ever have—so don't come asking me for another one."

Justin stumbles past me, crying.

"Go home, Sam," Chief Beaumont says. "That's it. No more dog-walking. I'll take the dogs home and see that you get the rest of your pay."

"But my customers need me."

"They'll have to work out something else." The look on his face says it all. He knows Justin wasn't lying about the teasing.

I stumble away, too. With every step, the voice in my head repeats over and over,

It wasn't all Justin's fault.... It wasn't all Justin's fault.... It wasn't all Justin's fault....

One mission occupies my mind as I bike the three miles home from CountryWood. Dropping my bike in the driveway, I race upstairs to my closet. My dog book feels like it weighs fifty pounds as I haul it to the trash can on the street. It's what started the whole thing. The trash haulers will be by soon. At the end of the day, the scrapbook will be rotting in a landfill.

Right where it belongs.

Chapter 25

Life doesn't make sense. No matter what happens, people crawl out of bed and go on living. Our place is a madhouse on Saturday. Grandma has gotten worse and Mom has to go talk to the doctor. Beth is getting ready for work. And Rosie is underfoot, as usual.

"Why don't you go see Bailey? She needs to finish your costumes."

"All done, and they're *bee-yoo-ti-ful.*"

"Yeah, *right.*"

Though Bailey has lost weight, she still isn't what I would call skinny. And something tells me getting thinner hasn't made her a better clothes designer.

It's after lunch before the house clears out. All last night and this morning, I haven't been able to stop thinking, *If only...*

If only Justin hadn't called me a loser.

If only he'd left me alone.

If only he'd become Bruno's alpha person.

I close the door to Mom's office and dial the number I've memorized. Numbly, I give Ms. Kendall the news about the puppy.

"I'm so sorry, Sam. As luck would have it, someone came in last night who's interested in the puppy. But..."

I'm not sure I want to hear what she has to say. Is she going to tell me she's reconsidered? That she's decided to do layaway? That she'll accept a nonrefundable deposit? Now that it's too late?

"Well, I think it was wonderful that you tried earning the money yourself. And we'll have a new puppy for you when you *do* get the money. But…"

That *but* again.

"Well, next time I expect you to come out and see the puppies. You know, a dog chooses the person as much as the person chooses the dog. We want our puppies to go to the right person." A pause. "I'll call the people and tell them the puppy is theirs." *Click.*

It's real. My puppy belongs to someone else.

I can't eat at supper.

"You coming down with something, Sam?" Mom feels my forehead. "Maybe you caught a chill in that thunderstorm. Your mattress is probably dry enough to bring back inside now. You sleep in the house tonight."

"Can't."

Mom, Beth, and Rosie look at me.

"What do you mean?" Mom says.

"I mean, I want to sleep outside." I get up from the table. "I'm going to go feed Max and Birdie now."

But when I reach the backyard, I don't head for the old barn. Instead, I straddle my bike and head down the county road. I ride toward CountryWood but don't stop there. I push my legs round and round. As my legs spin, the anger builds up inside me. Not at Justin this time. At myself.

Why did I tease him that way? Why didn't I just ignore him? It's all my fault.

Words pound in my head like a drum.

Failure.

Washout.

Bust.

Dud.

Loser.

The last word gets stuck.

Loser. Loser. Loser…

I screech to a stop. Legs putty. Shirt soaked. Skin wind-burned. Putting my rage dictionary back on its shelf, I turn my bike for home. My legs are burning by the time I reach Country-Wood, but there's still three miles to go. No choice but to keep pedaling.

It's almost dark when I put my bike in the garage. At the spigot back of the house, I wash my face with cold water. Drink a gallon as it streams onto the ground. Go to the barn to feed and water Birdie and Max. Birdie's chicks are growing fast, a couple even putting on pinfeathers. Before long, they'll be leaving the nest. Max empties his food dish and drains his water bowl. I refill it, watch him empty it again, and listen to him belch.

"Dumb old dog." I rub his head.

My body feels empty, like some monster leech has sucked the energy out of it. Dropping down on the ground, I lean against the barn. Exhausted. Max drops down beside me, grunting like dogs do when they're with their owner. Their alpha person.

I push stringy hair away and look into chestnut-brown eyes. He's here for me. He's *always* been here for me. Waiting.

"I'm sorry, Max."

I know he's just a dog, but a part of me believes Max understands.

Chapter 26

"Finally, good and dry. At least these hot days were good for something."

Mom helps me carry my mattress upstairs. A week has gone by since I lost my job, and I'm still sleeping outside. Chief Beaumont mailed the rest of my pay, but I haven't heard from any of my customers. I wasn't expecting to, really. Like the chief said, word gets around. They know I had a part in Bruno's death. I've been helping in the plant shed a lot because Mom checks on Grandma every day now. She had to be moved to a place that provides full-time care. I don't mind. I'm glad to have something to do.

Mom stretches sheets over the mattress and hands me a clean pillowcase. "Change out your pillowcase and you're all set." She smiles. "Bet you're anxious to get back to your own bed."

"Well, see, I'm going to sleep in the tent awhile longer. But thanks for the clean pillowcase. The other one is smelling pretty doggy."

Mom frowns. "Do we need to talk about something, Sammy? This isn't like you. What is it?"

"No, it's nothing. I, uh, I just like sleeping in the tent." I get the Mom look. Mouth a straight line. Eyes frozen in a stare. "It's—it's just that Beth will be taking the tent with her to Colorado, so this is my last chance."

"It's the puppy, isn't it? I know you had your heart set on buying it this summer." She blinks. "I still don't understand why it was so important to buy it now, but—"

"Nothing's wrong, Mom. Okay?"

She doesn't budge. Time for a diversion.

"Gotta get to the kitchen. My turn to help with supper. I'm, uh, I'm making a special dessert I learned from one of my customers at CountryWood."

"Dessert? But it's too hot to use the oven."

"Don't need to."

She smiles again. "I can hardly wait."

I hurry downstairs, hoping what I need is in the pantry and freezer.

Thank you, Mrs. Callahan!

Dessert is a huge hit. I explain that it's a traditional Irish dessert. Mom says she's going to keep ice cream and apple jelly around all the time. It's fun, laughing with Mom, Beth, and Rosie. But then they start talking about the things they're doing.

Moving to Colorado.

Entering the beauty pageant.

Making a big sale.

I can't wait to get away. Max greets me at the tent, tongue drooping a foot. Though daytime temperatures have dipped, it's still hot for late June. I change my pillowcase and crawl inside.

The night is peaceful. Crickets and frogs singing their night songs. Owls *swoosh*ing through the trees. Clouds playing tag with the moon. Max snoring.

I breath in deep. Exhale slowly. In time, darkness erases everything on my mental whiteboard.

Sleeping bag a sleeping bag.

Max's growl jolts me awake. He's at the door of the tent, trying to push through the mosquito netting. Then I smell it. Musk. The smell of a wild animal.

I grab the flashlight and my ball bat, unzip the door. Max knocks the flashlight and bat out of my hands. In the darkness, I can't find either one. But I don't need the flashlight to see what's happening. In the dim light, eyes are glowing. *Lots* of eyes.

I identify four sets of eyes surrounding us, four ringed tails shining in the moonlight. The marauding raccoons are back.

Birdie is awake, too. I can hear her in the nest, pushing four cheeping baby birds under her body for protection. Raccoons eat all kinds of things. Roots. Garbage. Pet food. Small mammals. Birds.

"Go away! Get back!" I run back and forth, waving my arms and yelling. Max barks, running at one raccoon, then another. Stopping to catch my breath, I see a huge set of eyes on one side of me, three smaller sets on the other. And then the huge set starts to get bigger. And bigger.

"Aww, man."

I've gotten between the mother raccoon and her babies. A stupid thing to do. A mother raccoon—any animal mother—is very protective of her young.

I run.

The raccoon is huge. Its gigantic shadow chases me, a shadow that's attached to a ring-tailed ball of claws and teeth. Then a bigger shadow runs it to the ground, a ferocious monster dog. Max snaps at the mother raccoon's tail until it runs off, the three smaller raccoons racing after it.

And just like that, the night is peaceful again.

"Woohoo!" I yell like a crazy person and do an Indian dance around the yard. "Max the warrior dog to the rescue! He saved us from the evil Fenrir!"

Max jumps around, too. Barking like he's gone mad.

"Sammy Smith—what is going on out here?" Mom stands at the corner of the barn, hands on hips. Beth is behind her, rubbing her eyes. "That yelling would wake the dead."

"The raccoons—Max chased off the raccoons."

"Cool." Beth raises a high five in my direction. "Going back to bed now...." She retreats into the shadows.

"That's good, Sammy." Mom's tolerant face makes a showing. Soft. Smiling. "But it's time you moved back into the house. You're wrecking my sleep. Now get your pillow and follow me."

"No."

"What?" Mom's angry face emerges. A traffic light, blinking red.

"What I mean is, I need to stay awhile longer." I'm not sure why, I just know I do. "Please, Mom. Just until Birdie's babies fly. Those raccoons might come back. I...I don't want to abandon her."

Mom sags, her exhausted face showing. "I swear, Sammy Smith. I don't know what's come over you this summer." She disappears around the barn, shaking her head.

I look at Max, who's taken up his post in front of Birdie's nest. Sitting erect. Shaggy mane encircling his neck. A stone lion.

"You're a warrior dog, Max." I pull him close and give him a hug. "A *real* hero."

We crawl back inside the tent. The battle won, we stretch out on a bed of goose down. The night erupts again. Frogs and crickets. Night birds. A noisy riot of sound. But Max and I don't care.

Sleeping bag a victory robe.

Chapter 27

It's the last Tuesday in June, and I'm sitting on Bailey's front porch. Minus Rosie. She and Mom went to Walmart to buy shoes for the pageant. Mootsies Tootsies for girls, white patent leather, on sale for $29.99. Plus tax. I was invited to go but declined. Big surprise.

I'm watching the cheer team do a new cheer, one cheerleaders did at the school Anise went to in the burbs.

> "Bang bang choo-choo train,
> Come on, girls, let's do this thang.
> I can't. Why not?
> I can't. Why not?
> 'Cause my back is aching,
> And my bra's too tight,
> And my body's shaking,
> From the left to the right,
> And my mama said my pants are too tight,
> But my boyfriend said they fit just right."

When they finish, they fall on the ground, a pile of giggles. I shake my head, smothering a grin.

They're going to get into so much trouble in middle school....

Bailey doesn't do the fake fat-girl thing anymore. She's just a regular girl. But some of her fashion sense has rubbed off on Anise and Yee. They both wear tie-dyed tees now and Converse shoes. Anise's are Chuck Taylor Thundercats. Yee's have Wonder Woman on them.

Yee sits down next to me, hair pulled back in a ponytail that swings when she talks. "They're building the dog park this weekend."

"I heard." Rosie gave me that news already. It seems Justin's mother needed more petunias, and Patty told Rosie. Of course.

"I figured you'd heard. The news about Bruno and your job is all over CountryWood."

I look at her. "So why'd you bring it up?"

"Because Anise and I organized a bunch of kids to help. Chief Beaumont's telling everyone the park was your idea, so I was hoping you would come. Bailey's biking out. We're getting her a gate pass so she can get in. She's going to meet up with us tomorrow about one o'clock."

Bailey's dream has come true. She gets to go to Country-Wood.

"That's great. That you're inviting Bailey, I mean." I stare at the ground like grass and dirt are the most fascinating things on the planet. Flick a pebble across the yard. Mumble, "I feel bad about Bruno."

"Yeah." Yee puts her hand on my arm. "Does it mean you won't get your dog? You know, because your job is over?"

"Sort of."

"Sorry."

I look at Yee's hand. At the color going up her neck to her cheeks. And grin.

She takes her hand away. "Hey, want to go to a movie this weekend?" Her ponytail flips. Her eyes laugh. "It's a sci-fi movie about big blue people with long cat tails that live on another planet. I could meet you down on the square. Anise is calling Gary, you know, that Townie who sat next to her in class. And Bailey's asking someone, too."

My heart thumps. "Sid?"

"No. She asked him first, but he can't. He's busy with this pageant thing."

I'm disappointed. I'd really like to see Sid.

"Well, I *would* like to see that movie." I retie shoelaces that don't need retying. Suck on a blade of grass. Say, "Yeah, I'd like to help with the dog park. It's the right thing to do. You know, for everybody."

"I'll let you know when the movie starts. You set it up with your mom to give you a ride to the Rialto."

"Yes, ma'am." I give her a salute.

She pretends to sneer and rejoins Anise and Bailey. A minute later, the shock wave hits.

Did I just make a date with a girl?

Bailey and I bike over to CountryWood the next afternoon to help with the dog run. She's dressed to impress. Retro plaid shorts she found at the Salvation Army store. A green shirt covered in eyes she drew with felt-tip markers, the letters *I C U* across the front. She's a chatterbox on the way, all excited about getting inside CountryWood. But once inside, she clams up. Mouth hermetically sealed.

I glance at her. "What is it?"

"I don't know." She eyes the bald yards and Lego houses. "Guess I just expected . . . *more*."

I just grin.

All kinds of people are at the corner lot where I walked the four dogs. Mr. P, Mrs. Callahan, and Professor Muller are sitting together in folding chairs under one of the trees. Mr. P and Mrs. Callahan brought refreshments for everyone. Greek shortbread cookies and Emerald Isle Tea.

"*Sammy . . .*" Mr. P. smiles when I walk up. "Come, you eat." He hands me two cookies.

"Oh, yes," Mrs. Callahan says, pushing a paper cup into my hand. "I'm so glad you could come."

I introduce Bailey to them, and she gets treats, too. She whispers, "It would be rude to refuse," to me as she accepts the cookies. I just grin. Some days are meant for celebrating, not dieting.

"Look . . ." Mr. P waves a hand toward the new dog park. "You see what you did, Sammy? The chief, he tells everyone it is your idea."

"Yes, it's thanks to you that we have this wonderful new place." Mrs. Callahan refills Bailey's and my cups with Emerald Isle Tea, which tastes like limeade. "And Mr. Muller is donating a park bench so we can sit and watch our dogs play together."

Professor Muller's knee is better. I learn that Mr. P is cleaning up his yard until his knee is fully healed and driving both Siegfried and Mrs. Callahan's dogs to the corner lot with Apollo to exercise.

"I run a dog taxi service," Mr. P says, laughing. "They hear my car in the driveway and come running to the front door. And my doctor, he says the fresh air is good for me."

"In another week, I'll be good as new," Professor Muller says, "so I can meet him here with Siegfried. The doctor says I am a model patient."

Big surprise. I notice he doesn't look so wooden—softer, somehow. They all look happier, so I don't feel too bad about losing my job anymore.

Bailey joins up with Yee and Anise. I pick up a shovel and veer off, looking for someone else.

Justin is already digging holes for the fence posts. I walk up next to him. He's surprised to see me.

I nod. He nods back. We go to work.

Chapter 28

It's my second shower of the day. After the first one, I helped Mom in the garden. Turning over ground for a new perennial she wants to try. Misting annuals in the shed, which was a sauna. And brushing Max, who had turned to Velcro again—collecting grass and sticks like they were priceless objects. By the time I finished with him, I had transformed to a werewolf.

Someone pounds on the bathroom door.

"I'm not done!"

"Well, *get* done!" Beth yells. "Mom got a call from a customer and needs to deliver plants. She's taking Rosie with her, so I'm your ride to the movie. And I can't be late 'cause the vet's doing surgery on a horse and I get to watch."

Most sisters go nuts about lipstick and clothes. I get a mad scientist.

"Five minutes!"

"Make it three!"

I brush the waves in my hair as smooth as I can. Pull clothes onto a partially wet body. Tie shoelaces. Race downstairs. Beth is at the car, putting air in the tires again.

Great. With my luck, we'll blow a tire on the way.

Since it's only a ten-minute drive to town, I put my faith in rubber trees and climb into the passenger seat.

"Isn't Bailey going?" Beth asks. "She could ride with us."

"Yeah, but she went into town early. You know, to shop and stuff."

Beth maneuvers around the town square, crowded with

shoppers and moviegoers. It's the last Saturday before July Fourth, so the stores are busy and parking is tight.

"What's the name of this movie?" She wheels her Subaru around a third time, scanning for a parking space.

"Don't remember." I spot the cheerleading squad walking up the block. "Hey, look, just stop here and I'll walk."

"Okay, okay. Geez, what's with you? The feature doesn't start for another thirty minutes."

"Thought you had to operate on a horse."

"The clinic's five minutes away, Sammy."

My hands are so sweaty, I can't grip the door handle. Finally, the door yields. Outside, I hesitate. Look at Beth. Say, "Do, uh, do I have swag?"

"Swag?"

"Yeah, you know. Look good."

"Aha." She gives me a big grin, dimpled. "You're meeting a girl, aren't you?"

"Aww, man." I slam the car door.

"Wait." Beth leans across the seat and talks through the window. "Yeah, you do look big-city, but…" She motions to me to get back in the car.

But? I crawl into the passenger seat. Beth drives around the square again, mouth opening and closing like she's a fish out of water, gulping air.

"What *is* it, Beth?"

"I just never thought this job would fall to me." She sighs. Takes a deep breath. Says, "All right, here's the CliffsNotes version for dating. Holding hands is cool. A peck on the lips, cool— but not on the first date. Maybe not even the second."

"A peck?"

"Like Grandma gives us." She gives the air a smooching kiss. "And the girl needs to let you know when it's okay."

"She tells you to kiss her?"

"No. You have to read between the lines."

Great. I'm back to being a mind reader.

"And *no* making out."

"Wait up. What's that involve…exactly?"

"Tongue."

Tongue? I envision Max's long tongue, drooling slime.

"Do not even think of going beyond tongue."

"Don't worry, I'm not."

"And date one girl at a time. You start playing the field, you'll be considered promiscuous." Hazel eyes drill a hole in me. "You know what that means?"

"I watch TV, Beth."

"Good. The same works for girls, too. So if you value your reputation, think smart." She pulls to a stop in front of the theater. Again. "That about covers it. Now, go have a good time."

Good time? I'm afraid to get out of the car.

"One more question. Do I pay her way?"

"Not on a first date or when you're meeting up in a gang. If you want to buy her popcorn or a Coke on the second or third date, that's cool. And if you ask her someplace special and it's just the two of you, then yeah, you pay the whole works. But I wouldn't be in a hurry to get there." She lowers her voice and whispers like she's sharing a secret with me. "Dream big, Sammy. Long-term. For me, that's college. You need to think that way, too."

I groan my reply. My dreams are trash in a landfill.

"Now, go. I'll pick you up at four." She gives me a grin and a knuckle bump.

I watch Beth drive off. Try to remember the rules. Stumble on words like *peck* and *tongue. Promiscuous.*

"*Sammy*—" Yee's wearing a yellow shirt and matching shorts. "Hurry up, I'm holding us a place in line." She waves me toward the ticket booth, long hair glistening like she's brushed it a hundred times.

Why am I sweating? I don't need to remember the rules. Yee probably had them memorized by the time she registered for kindergarten.

I run.

Chapter 29

Rosie does a dress rehearsal on the Sunday before the pageant, which is on July 14. Only a week away. I can't believe how fast summer is going.

Beth thought a practice would help Rosie relax. Yee, Anise, and Bailey came over to help Rosie get ready. They're all upstairs now, chattering like crows in a corn patch. I'm sitting downstairs in the living room. Waiting.

The cheerleading squad comes downstairs to wait with me for Rosie's grand entrance, which had to be delayed. Nerves reached Rosie's bladder and tights had to be removed so she could pee.

More waiting and fidgeting. Bailey brings up Bruno.

"I bet his dad buys him another dog. And this one will cost *five* hundred big ones."

"He really does spoil Justin." Anise gives her head a shake. "And his little sister, too. Their stuff takes up half their garage, and their basement, too, I hear."

"People have different ways of showing their love." Yee lets out a long sigh. "My parents burn incense to the ancestors when I bring home an A."

The others laugh, but I hang on to Yee's words for a while.

"Justin told Chief Beaumont he doesn't want another dog," Anise says. "I saw him ride his bike over to the chief's house one afternoon. That's when he told him."

"And of course, you were just close enough to overhear them," Yee says, looking all-knowing.

"I made sure of it." Anise gives her a smug grin. "Anyway, I guess Justin's dad made him go apologize to the chief for the mess he made. And when the chief told him he would do better with the next dog, Justin said he didn't want one."

"Why?" Bailey says.

" 'Cause he really loved Bruno," I say. I'm remembering the way Justin cried when Bruno died.

"He told you that?" Yee's eyes telegraph she's not convinced.

"Sort of."

Mom and Beth come in and announce that the practice is about to begin. When Rosie walks down the stairs, I can hardly believe it's my bratty little sister. Shining like gold, her hair is braided around her head like Princess Leia's in *Star Wars*. And the costume Bailey designed looks elegant. Professionally made. When Rosie changes into her Chippewa costume and does her modern dance, everyone stands. Applauding.

"Thanks." I smile at the cheerleading squad as they leave. "I owe you. Big-time."

"Don't worry." Yee grins. "I won't let you forget."

"You can double that," Anise says.

"Triple it," Bailey says.

They leave in a troop, giggling like they know something I don't.

I stop Rosie as she's going upstairs to change. "What about the third costume? You know, the glittery one for when you win the tiara." In spite of Sid's talk with Rosie, I know she thought she still had a chance to win.

"Well, I talked to Bailey and Yee and Anise and, and... I decided that was dumb." Serious eyes match the serious words. "I may not win, but it's okay 'cause this has been the best summer ever."

Where did the brat who whines all the time go?

"Win or lose, you're a princess, Rosie. You look... *splendid*."

Chapter 30

On Tuesday night, Mom and Beth go at it again, their angry voices booming up the stairs. I perch on the top step, listening.

"Those tires aren't safe. You need new ones."

"I know, Mom. Soon as I can, I'll get them."

"I could scrape up a *little* to help out, but..."

"Chill out, Mom. I can take care of it myself. Remember, I have a part-time job lined up."

"Still, it's a long way to Colorado."

"These tires will get me there."

Silence signals a truce. It's safe to go downstairs.

"Oh, morning, Sammy." Mom turns as I walk into the room. "When you're through with breakfast, I could use some help. Meet me in the shed?"

"Okay."

I put a frozen waffle in the toaster and take butter and jelly from the refrigerator. "Heard you and Mom talking. You know, 'bout tires." I glance at Beth out of the corner of my eye. "You *do* need some new ones."

"Like I don't know that." Beth snorts. "But it just isn't gonna happen. Not unless you know someone with deep pockets."

"Yeah, well, maybe I do."

"Oh, yeah?" A cynical laugh replaces the snorting. "Who?"

"Me." I spread a waffle with butter and grape jelly.

"*Right*. Help me with something." Beth looks to the side, pretending she's trying to remember something. "Didn't you hit me up for a loan a few weeks ago?"

"Got a job, remember?"

She stops talking and stares at me. "You offering to loan me what you made?"

"That, and the other ninety I already had saved." I lick jelly off the spoon. "Got a hundred sixty-five bucks. Well, a hundred fifty. Spent some at the movies and might need a little more before summer's over. Not enough for four new tires, but you could get retreads."

Hazel-colored eyes glisten. "Hold up." She wipes her eyes with her sleeve. "You've been saving up to buy that puppy from Kendall's Kennels. What happened?"

"She's already sold the last one. But it's okay."

Beth looks at me. "Okay?"

I tell her about Justin. How he called me a loser. How I was going to make *him* the loser. How Siegfried got hurt. Twice. How Bruno died.

"Mrs. Kendall said she admired me for earning my own money for a puppy, but..." A huge lump forms in my throat. "But I don't feel very admirable. I'd really like to give you the money for the tires."

She sits down with me and eats jelly off a spoon. "It'll be a loan. I'll pay you back as soon as I can and you can keep adding to it until you have enough to buy a puppy. Look at it as a puppy on installments."

"Well, uh, I was thinking about other kinds of payback?"

Her eyes narrow to slits. "Like what?"

The lump in my throat dissolves. Words flood out. "It's Mom. She's going to expect me to be just like you, and I'm not. I can never be as smart as you. And Rosie, she's always doing these dumb things, asking these dumb questions. And she's getting to be a real wiseass. I won't know how to keep her out of trouble. And then there's..."

Beth waits.

I sigh. "Girls. I think I'm going to have a lot of questions about girls. You know, the kind you can't ask your mom?"

Beth laughs so hard, tears come to her eyes. "I'm only a

phone call away. And my advice is free, so I *will* pay you back eventually. But it may take a while."

"Cool."

"And stop putting yourself down, you're a smart guy." She gives me a smothering hug. "You'll do just fine after I'm gone. And one day, you'll get your puppy. I can feel it in my bones."

"Yeah?"

"Yeah."

Aww, man. Now I wish I hadn't thrown my scrapbook away.

Chapter 31

July 14. Pageant day, and it starts early. Crack-of-dawn early: 5:30 AM. Contestants have to arrive ahead of time to sign in and get set up in the dressing room. Mom and Beth carry Rosie's clothes downstairs, covered in plastic trash bags that Beth converted to garment bags. I'm the pack mule that hauls everything outside to Mom's van.

"Don't bend them, Sammy," Rosie says, panic in her voice. "Don't bend my costumes."

We're all attending, including the cheerleading squad. Bailey, Anise, and Yee are biking to the hotel together. Beth took off from work for the big day. Mom strung a makeshift banner across the Smith's Flower Shed sign that reads, ATTENDING PRINCESS PAGEANT AT MIDWEST JEWEL INN TODAY—SALE ON PETUNIAS STARTING TOMORROW. I'm staying behind to take care of Max, Birdie, and the days of the week. I'll bike over later when the pageant officially begins. The only one who won't be going is Grandma. That invisible curtain in front of her has closed completely. She doesn't recognize anyone anymore.

"I think that's everything," Beth says.

I pull Rosie aside and say, "Be cool. Those rich kids don't have a thing on you."

"True dat." She gives me a fist bump.

Mom raises an eyebrow at me.

"Hey, she didn't learn that from me."

"Let's roll!" Beth yells from the driver's seat.

"Wait, we forgot something." Mom looks at me. "Sid called. He wants to borrow your dog book."

"I...I threw it away."

"What?" Mom's eyes open wide. "But you worked years on that scrapbook. Why would you throw it away?"

"No, *wait.*" Rosie races upstairs and returns with my scrapbook under an arm. "I rescued it."

"Geez, Rosie." The three-ring binder is like an old friend I've found again.

"Want me to give it to Sid?" Beth says, grinning.

"No, I'll, uh, I'll bring it when I come."

I watch my family disappear down the road, all of them so excited, and feel sad. Come fall, another of us will be gone. First, Dad, then Grandpa, and now Grandma's lost.

Vanishing, like ticks of a clock.

A door slams across the road. I watch Bailey run to her bike. See Yee and Anise pull into her driveway. Wave as they all push off.

Anise yells, "Bike over with us!"

"Later. I've got chores first."

"Don't be late." Yee's ponytail swishes back and forth like a thick rope. "Watch the clock."

"Plenty of time." At the curve in the road, they all turn and wave at me.

I smile. The thing about clocks is one tick follows another. New ones replace those that die away.

It's quiet...for about ten seconds. Then seven loud cats gather in a horde, mingling around my legs, demanding food. Smudges of yellow and blue and red remain, but nothing that's readable. Still, I know every one of them by name. Laying my dog book on the porch, I fill water bowls and food dishes.

After the cats are happy, I head for the barn. Looking like a stone lion, Max sits in front of Birdie's nest. Where the nest *used* to be. It now lies on the ground, the mud cement holding bits and pieces of sticks and straw broken into jagged clumps.

"What happened, Max?"

Birds answer for him. Lots of birds. Birdie and her brood have taken to the treetops.

"Come on, Max, time to go home. Plenty of time to clean up this other stuff later." Carrying his food and water dish, I walk back to the house. In front of me, our shadows point the way.

For the first time in weeks, Max chomps his Dog Chow on the back porch. He lets out a huge burp when he's finished and settles down next to me on the stoop. Grunting like a bear settling in for the long winter.

Back to normal.

We listen to birdcalls. Watch the days of the week chase grasshoppers and butterflies. Feel a cool breeze blowing in from the south, a sign of rain. It feels good.

Reaching for my scrapbook, I open the cover and look through its pages. Twice I threw the book away, and twice it came back to me. Is that a sign, too? Will one of the dogs inside its pages choose me one day? As I flip the pages, the dogs blend into one. Big and little. Light and dark. Shaggy and short haired.

And then I get it—*really* get it. All this time, a dog already had chosen me.

I lay the book aside and scratch Max's shaggy head. The clock ticks. Nothing lasts forever. One day, Max will leave me, too.

But not yet. *Please*, not yet....